Dragonbound VII

Gold Dragon

Rebecca Shelley

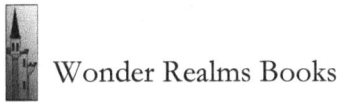 Wonder Realms Books

Cover art © Starblue | Dreamstime.com
Interior art © Rocich | Dreamstime.com

ISBN-13: 978-0692412152
ISBN-10: 0692412158

Published by Wonder Realms Books

To dragon lore expert Jessica Scott.

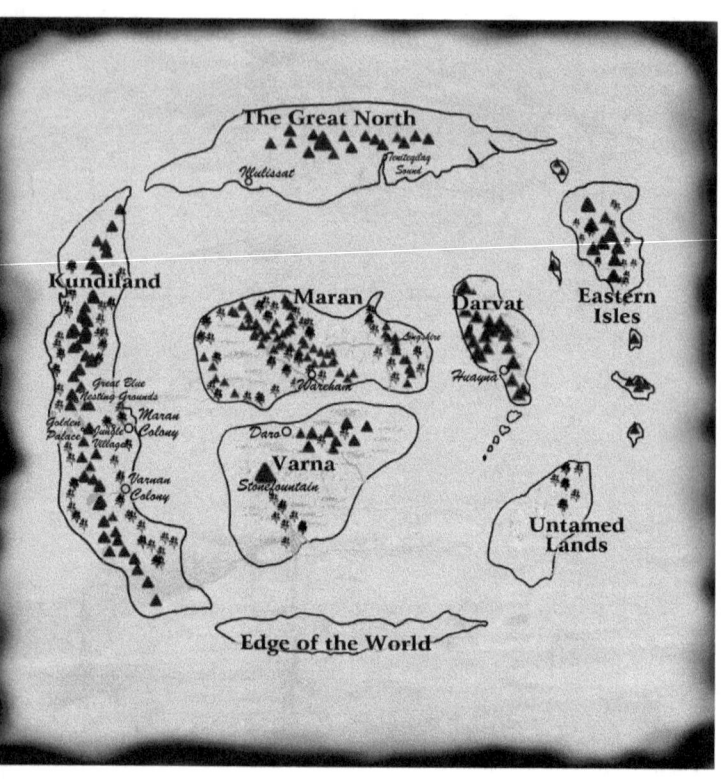

Dragonbound

Dragonbound: Blue Dragon
Dragonbound II: White Dragon
Dragonbound III: Copper Dragon
Dragonbound IV: Red Dragon
Dragonbound V: Silver Dragon
Dragonbund VI: Green Dragon
Dragonbound VII: Gold Dragon
Dragonbound VIII: Black Dragon

Prologue

I have spent my life living peacefully, caring for the dragons and other creatures around me, wanting for nothing, and needing nothing more than I have: a home, a beautiful wife, two incredible sons, and a dragon companion who has through the last five hundred years been a second heartbeat to mine, a mind to match my own, a friend, and a councilor. I never could have dreamed that my life could change so quickly from happiness to torment. Surely this is just a nightmare from which I will wake and see a golden sunrise over the steamy jungle.

Amar

Chapter One

Amar stood with his hands on the smooth golden windowsill and watched the rising sun chase the fog off the treetops below. Behind him, Rajahansa snorted in his sleep and shifted. He'd wake soon, and Amar's moments of mental freedom would end. He thought about casting himself out the window, but the young gold dragons on either side of him would grab him once again the moment he put his first foot up on the windowsill. Rajahansa wasn't taking any chances with his life.

The arms of the mountains reached out in a bowl shape, surrounding the jungle valley below. As daylight lit the sky, the circle of blue dragons perched along the mountain cliffs became visible. They'd been there at sunset, and they were still there now. Rajahansa would be furious when he woke. Thank the fountain, Kanvar had gotten Amar's message from Tana. Amar was confident the blue dragons would never let Rajahansa leave the palace again.

On the jungle floor, the Black River wound its way through the trees, flowing down the mountains and out past the jungle village to the ocean beyond. Rajahansa's scouts had confirmed the arrival of the human armies.

Did you think you could hide from them forever? Khalid's voice like sludge swept through Amar's mind. *Grandson, really, there is only one solution to the human problem.*

Amar blocked Khalid's destructive thoughts that came to his mind from the waking Rajahansa's. If only Rajahansa had not let himself be seduced by the tyrant, things would be different. Yes, the humans would still come, but the world was a big place and dragons could fly to places human armies would never reach.

You would run and hide like a dung beetle? Rajahansa mocked him.

"This conflict is pointless. The world is big enough for all of us." Amar turned from the window to face his dragon. Rajahansa lay curled in the center of the chamber. His golden plates shone in the pale morning light from the window. He had scars now that he'd never had before, scars Kanvar's dragon had given him on the day Kanvar had bonded, and others Anilon had inflicted. Rajahansa had not forgotten that, nor forgiven it. Amar had been foolish to think that he would.

The smell of breakfast cooking in the palace kitchens lingered on the air. Bellori, the young gold dragon in charge of serving food to the king, would bring it soon: roasted bovinder for Rajahansa, fruit and honeyed milk for Amar. Just like every other morning . . . and not.

You are right, Amar. Today will be a day remembered in the history of the world forever as the day you and I rose to greatness and power. Rajahansa stood, spread his wings, and shook away the sleep.

"If you try for Stonefountain, today will be the day the blue dragons kill us. Have no doubt, Rajahansa. They will not let Khalid return to this world."

Khalid's dark laughter pulsed through Amar's shields. Khalid said something to Rajahansa, but Amar refused to hear it. He would not listen to Khalid's lies and promises.

You're a fool, Rajahansa told Amar. *Stonefountain has had a thousand years to regain its power, a thousand years worth of souls added to replace those that were torn from it. You cannot deny this truth. It is evident in the seed of your blood. Five hundred years you tried to have Naga children and failed. It is Stonefountain that imbues the Nagas with power. Wounded, it could bring precious few Nagas to life. Now look, in one generation: Karishi, Rajan, Devaj, Kanvar, Tana, Aadi, and Denali. Our numbers have more than doubled. It is the fountain itself that calls us to it. It's time that true civilization is restored.*

"I hear Khalid's voice in your words. The old civilization was corrupt and evil. It should be purged from memory, not restored."

Rajahansa bared his teeth and roared at Amar. *Do not anger me or I'll let Khalid take your mind again. I know how much you enjoy his company.*

Amar shuddered. Khalid and Rajahansa together could so easily tear through his shields, and when they did, Khalid was never gentle. Amar's stomach twisted and the smell of food sickened him suddenly. He was a prisoner here in the palace where he'd always been safe before—his mind bound and tormented by his enemies beyond any physical punishment a human jailor could contrive. He turned back to the window, hands shaking. "Rajahansa, I beg you one more time. Rid your mind of this connection to Khalid. Before you do anything more, sever the link and think freely again for a while."

Rajahansa knocked him across the room, so he hit the floor and slid up against the wall. *Silence! You sicken me.*

"The feeling is mutual."

Rajahansa gave him a mental slap and would have turned Khalid loose on him again, but a pair of gold dragons swooped in through the window and landed.

Your Majesty, the older of the two dragons said, bowing. *The human armies are moving up the river toward the village, half in boats and half on land. They have engaged with the dragon army.*

So be it, Rajahansa said. *The humans think they can win, but they will fail.*

We spotted a flight of blue dragons out by the coast, the scout said.

Good. If the humans and blues fight each other, all the better for us. Gather all the gold dragons and be ready to fight. The blues will not hold us here. Our destiny awaits elsewhere. Rajahansa shooed the scouts away and called for Bellori to bring breakfast.

Amar remained where he'd been thrown. If there was anything he could do to fight Rajahansa, surely he would do it, but the power was beyond him now. His best hope was to remain quiet and unnoticed so Rajahansa and Khalid would leave him alone.

Majesty, Bellori's gentle thoughts stirred him sometime later. *Your breakfast.* Bellori put a tray of sweet bread, fruit, and honeyed milk on the ground beside him and eased him up to sit with his back against the wall.

"I'm not hungry." He pushed away the cup of milk Bellori held out to him and noticed that Rajahansa had already eaten and left the chamber. Amar's two dragon guards still flanked the window.

You must be; you didn't eat last night, Bellori said.

Bellori. Amar rubbed the young dragon's neck while whispering into his mind. *I don't want you to fight today. Leave the palace now. Rajahansa expects you to fly back and forth between here and the herds you keep. He won't question you leaving the palace. You're small enough to get down below the canopy. Go down, and stay down, no matter what happens up here. Promise me you will.*

Bellori quivered. *Rajahansa will kill me.*

No. He and I are leaving today. He won't even notice. Go back to the kitchens now then get away while no one is looking. Amar patted Bellori and urged him to go.

I will on one condition, Bellori said. *You eat your breakfast.*

Amar chuckled and took the cup of milk. "If you insist."

I do. Bellori bowed, glanced nervously over his shoulder at the two dragon guards at the window, then slid out of the room.

Amar took a sip of the honey-sweetened milk, but the sudden roar of the dragon guards tumbled the cup from his hand. Not just the two guards in this chamber, but dragons at each of the windows let out a roar of alarm. Amar jumped to his feet and watched as what had to be every adult dragon of the blue dragon pride closed in on the palace. The gold dragon defenders took to the air to stop them. Rajahansa stormed into the chamber. *On my neck, now!* he ordered Amar.

Amar took a deep breath. *Please, Kanvar*, he thought as he climbed onto Rajahansa's neck. *Don't let me down.*

Kanvar will not stop us, Rajahansa spit into his mind. *Don't even try to contact him. You know I'll just block you.*

Amar flinched as Rajahansa lifted his head, locking the plate over Amar to hold him in place. Rajahansa climbed onto the window sill and lifted his wings, ready to launch into the air the moment the gold dragons managed to punch a hole in the circle of attacking blues. Amar blinked. Something was wrong. The blues were not in a retaining circle but were driving straight for the palace in a wedge-shaped formation. The new tactic took the gold dragons off guard, scattering them like butterflies in the wind.

Seeing his chance to break free, Rajahansa roared and took to the air. He need only fly to one side or other of the wedge and he'd be gone. Haidar and Liander astride their dragons came up on either side of him as the full force of the blue dragons headed toward them.

The gold dragons reformed and descended on the wedge, filling the air with their joy breath, but the blue dragons ignored them. They breathed no fire and made no move against the golds. They're holding their breath, Amar realized, so the joy breath won't affect them. Rajahansa dove low and made a break for the coast, followed by Haidar and Liander. Blue fire shot up from beneath him, burning his belly. Amar looked down and saw five of the largest and fiercest blue dragons launch up from the top of the canopy where they had been waiting. Amar's heart beat to match the flap of wings as the blue dragons closed the narrow gap. I'm going to die, he realized. He'd been waiting for this, but the shock of it stole his breath, and all at once he didn't want to die, though he knew he had to. He expected the blue dragons to hit the golds' underbellies with claws and teeth as they usually did, but the blues came up level with the golds instead.

The sudden shriek of singing stones sliced through Amar's mind. The pain was so surprising and intense he could hardly see to realize that the blue dragon which had risen up beside him was carrying dragon hunters in its claws. Amar barely recognized Qadim—the leader of the dragon hunter jati, a man he'd hunted and feasted with many times in the past, an old man with gray hair and muscles like jungle vines—before Qadim's crossbow bolt hit him in the right shoulder. A second bolt from another dragon hunter took him in the left.

"No!" Tana's voice called out from somewhere. "You promised to only shoot his dragon."

Amar choked as the pain from the wounds seized him, and Rajahansa faltered in flight. Qadim's triumphant smirk filled Amar's vision. Two bolts to the dragon's wings would not be enough to stop Rajahansa's flight. Qadim had shot Amar instead, and those wounds tore through Rajahansa's shoulders, crippling his flight.

In a burst of desperation, Rajahansa wheeled back to the palace.

But why? Amar wondered. Those same two bolts could have pierced his heart and ended it simply and painlessly. But Qadim didn't want Amar to die quickly and painlessly. That had to be it. Amar had made a fool of Qadim, and Qadim wanted to make Amar pay for it slowly and painfully. He wanted Amar to know who had come to kill him.

Rajahansa landed in the central chamber with Haidar beside him.

Haidar's dragon collapsed the moment he set down. Blood flowed from a hole in the dragon's heart where a crossbow bolt had hit Haidar. Amar could see no sign of Liander and his dragon. They must have fallen to the dragon hunters before reaching the palace.

Realizing what a vulnerability Amar was to him, Rajahansa tore Amar from his neck and thrust him behind as the five blue dragons deposited two dragon hunters each into the palace. A sixth dragon set Tana and General Chandran down. Amar lost sight of them as Rajahansa tore into the dragon hunters with joy breath, teeth, and tail. He fought for his life.

Amar stumbled against a pillar as sword strokes and crossbow bolts hit Rajahansa and manifested on Amar's body as well. Amar caught his breath. They were purposely making this as painful as they could.

"Your Majesty." Tana raced around Rajahansa and caught him as he fell. Blood from his flesh slicked her hands and armor as she eased him to the ground. Strange, so strange, she pressed a little silver decanter against his wounds so blood gushed into it. She swirled the liquid in the decanter and pressed it to his lips. "Drink, Majesty, quickly."

He opened his mouth to protest that he had no strength left to drink anything. "I'm dying, let me go," he tried to say, but a torrent of blood filled his mouth. Blood like coppery death and . . . gold. He swallowed, unable to do anything else to keep from drowning in the blood.

Tana snapped the decanter closed, went to the window, and hurled it out. The air rippled as a young gold dragon caught it and flew away.

Amar shook his head. What had he seen, what was going on? Everything was blood and pain, Rajahansa's roar and the shouts of dragon hunters. Crossbow bolts peppered Rajahansa. Swords cut him. The dragon hunters had covered their mouths and noses with cloth so the joy breath did no good. Amar felt each burning wound as they cut Rajahansa down.

Amar's breath gurgled in his throat. Had they hit Rajahansa's lungs? He could not breathe. Something green crawled in through the window. A moment later Vasanti gazed down at him, her dragonstone glowing green, but Amar could not hear her thoughts through the shriek of the singing stones. She tore the crossbow bolts from his shoulders and licked him, slathering his body with saliva. He coughed to clear his throat and draw in breath as Vasanti snatching him and Tana up together in her tail. She raced toward the window just as a spear slammed through Rajahansa's heart.

No! Rajahansa screamed with his dying thought. *Khalid, you promised me victory.*

Khalid's mocking laugh flashed back at him. *I will have victory, Rajahansa, just not with you. Did you really think I'd take a link with a dragon as strong-willed as yourself? You who would betray and chain your own Naga? No, never. I need a young dragon I can control. Do not fear; you have played the part I planned for you all along, distracting the humans. I will rise this day, despite your death. Devaj is already on his way to me.*

Khalid's power abandoned Rajahansa's soul, and it tore from his body as the spear hit his heart.

Amar screamed in agony as Rajahansa was sliced from his mind and body, leaving him hollow, empty, and dead. And not dead.

Amar gasped.

The green dragon's poison seeped past his bloody clothes into his skin, paralyzing him as the dragon carried him and Tana out the palace window and down the cliff face. Above them, the dragon hunters shouted and shot down at them. The Great Green dragon launched from the side of the cliff and spread her forelegs and back legs so the wind billowed into her flaps of skin between them, carrying her in a majestic glide away from the palace and out of range of the crossbows.

Dragons filled the air with blue fire and golden sparkles, but none of the fighting dragons paid any attention to the lone green dragon as she dropped toward the trees.

Tana clung to Amar in a tight hug, made tighter by the dragon's tail wrapped around the two of them. Tana's cheek nestle against his neck, hot against his skin as the dragon floated down to the trees and dug its claws into the trunk of one of the giants that poked its crown up above the other trees. That stopped them with a jerk, and the tail that held Amar and Tana lashed back and forth, jolting them.

Amar cried out at the jolt, but the sharp pain of his wounds seeped away as the dragon saliva did its work to heal them, leaving behind an ache in his body and an even heavier ache in his soul where Rajahansa had been.

Vasanti raced down the tree trunk, getting as much distance as she could between her and the dragon hunters.

Amar's mind tumbled with confusion and pain from the singing stones. He was alive, paralyzed by Vasanti's poison, but alive. Yet, it couldn't be. Rajahansa was dead, no doubt about that. Dead, and Amar could feel the emptiness inside himself trying to consume him. But Amar lived, breathed, ached.

"I'm alive," he said, his voice ragged to his own ears. Leaves and branches flashed past, and the world spun as Vasanti climbed down, head down, holding Tana and Amar upside down as well. Easy for a green dragon. Dizzying for the Nagas. Amar's stomach twisted around itself as Vasanti suddenly came up right and launched from one tree branch to glide to another tree. Gold dragon flight was smooth and beautiful, this was sheer chaos. Tana whooped with delight as her dragon glided between trees again and then launched one more time down to land on the jungle floor.

"Why am I alive?" Amar said as soon as his head stopped spinning from Vasanti's acrobatics.

"It's all right." Tana's arms were around him as if it were she who held him up as the Great Green dragon sped through the underbrush, unhindered by plant or animal. "You'll see in just a moment as soon as we get clear of the singing stones."

"Where's Kanvar?" Amar asked. His mouth, at least, could move, even though nothing else could. "Is he safe?

Those dragon hunters tried to kill you even though you brought them to the palace."

"Yes, of course. Vasanti and I planned for that. Kanvar made a deal with Chandran to stay out of the fighting. He's all right."

Amar swallowed. His head throbbed, but the song of the singing stones faded as Vasanti left the battle behind. Then there was just silence in his head. Empty silence. And then a voice.

> *Nikeron the Brave*
> *Five times blest by Stonefountain*
> *Five times his life he gave to save his people*
> *Five times he lived again*
> *Rebirthed by those who loved him*
> *Snatched from the pit of death by blood*
> *Given freely*
> *This is his tale I tell you*
> *A ballad beyond compare*
> *None has lived before or since as great as he...*

Until now. Amar, my king. Please accept my bond. I know you were given no choice, and that is a sin, but Kanvar and I could not bear to see you slaughtered. This world needs you yet alive.

Bensharie? Amar said. The warmth of pure gold spread through him as the new bond took him. For a moment he felt young again, a child guided by Parmver's hand through the Bonding Ceremony. How blest and full and joyous that day had been. He and Rajahansa had been perfect for each other, so perfect. Then the smell of blood and the dizzying lash of the Great Green dragon's tail that carried him, snapped Amar back to the present. Rajahansa was dead, gone, seduced by Khalid, used, and discarded. And Devaj . . . Devaj had been Khalid's target all along. Devaj, already on his way to Stonefountain. The full horror of that realization struck Amar like the spear blow that had killed Rajahansa. Devaj, Amar's son, his oldest son, would fall to Khalid instead of him. The darkness of that thought was too much to bear.

Kanvar, he screamed. *Kanvar, Khalid is forcing Devaj to Stonefountain. Fly, fly, and stop him. Go, save your brother, please. There's nothing I can do.* Paralyzed, stuck below the canopy with the green dragon, Amar was helpless to stop Devaj. Khalid had planned his strategy well, hiding his true intent.

You're alive. Kanvar's relieved thoughts tumbled back to him.

Yes. Go save Devaj.

Kill him, you mean?

No, stop him. Break Khalid's hold on him. Elkantran isn't like Rajahansa. Khalid must be controlling them both. If you can break through Khalid's shields, it will be the three of you against him. Amar could not bring himself to command Devaj's death. His own, yes, if it meant stopping Khalid. His son's death, no. It could not be.

Four against Khalid, Dharanidhar rumbled. *Don't not forget me.*

Yes, four. Go, fly. Amar felt Dharanidhar launch into the air, straining his aching wings against the sky.

I will meet you at Vasanti's lair, Bensharie said when Amar's mind turned back from Kanvar's. *Your Majesty, I am honored to be your dragon.*

The honor is mine, Amar said, tears trickling down his face. He was happy to have Bensharie with him, but he could not subdue his regret that Devaj would face Khalid instead of him.

Chapter Two

Kanvar loaded his crossbow while Dharanidhar flew fast
and furious, wings beating hard, both knowing they'd regret
the exertion later, but later wouldn't matter if they lost
Devaj to Khalid. In his mind, Kanvar calculated the distance and direction. Devaj had been on the western coast
of Kundiland at the new village. If he'd started at first light,
he'd be close to the eastern coast by now. Kanvar was
already on the coast. Flying high to stay out of range of the
humans, he'd been sweeping back and forth along the edge
of the water just in case Rajahansa had broken free from
the siege of the palace. That put Kanvar in the perfect
position to intercept Devaj. He just hoped his father was
right and he and Dharanidhar would be strong enough to
break Khalid's hold on Devaj.

All this time your brother was his main target, Dharanidhar fumed. *Khalid fooled us with so much mayhem at the palace, so much hurt and suffering. We have Akshara's memories of Khalid, but that's all they are, memories fogged by a thousand years. That's nothing like living through wickedness. We should have seen his plans, should have guessed his intent, and we didn't. Akshara counted on us, and we've failed him.*

Not yet we haven't. Kanvar swept his gaze across the horizon, looking for the tell-tale gold ripple of dragon flight. It had to be a sunny day today, didn't it? He'd never wished for cloud cover so much in his life. It was near impossible for one man and a dragon to cover the entire Kundiland coastline looking for one other dragon and man.

Stop looking for ripples and look for Devaj. He'll be visible even if Elkatran is not, Dharanidhar said.

Kanvar gritted his teeth. The hot wind blew across his face. *He wears golden robes, has golden hair and sun-bronzed skin. He'll blend in to the hot sun almost as much as his dragon.*

That's why I'm flying high. You can see him below us against the contrast of the green jungle rather than the brightness of the sun in the sky.

Kanvar's eyes stung from the wind in his face and from looking across such a wide expanse of land. Far below, the human soldiers and dragon hunters battled their way upriver toward the palace. Thank the fountain, his father was no longer there. It seemed almost too good to be true that Amar was now free from Rajahansa and alive.

Brave Bensharie to risk a link with the dying king. Kanvar would have been overjoyed if the fear for Devaj and the safety of the human world did not overshadow it.

Try calling him, Dharanidhar said. *Perhaps you can feel him with your mind better than you can see him with your eyes.*

Devaj! Kanvar called out. *Devaj!*

For a flash moment he felt his brother's mind, but a shield went up, and he lost contact. Kanvar swore and urged Dharanidhar in the direction he'd felt.

Dharanidhar wheeled back around toward the Maran Colony. *But he can't be coming this way. With the whole coast clear, why would he risk coming anywhere near the human army?*

I don't know. Kanvar's shoulders tensed with fear, and his chest tightened. He wanted to stay well out of range of the singing stones and ballistae.

Another of Khalid's tricks, do you suppose? Dhar rumbled.

Most likely.

Dhar swept high above the colony and back toward the mountains. Up ahead, Kanvar spotted the rocky peak that had torn Dharanidhar from the sky on the day he and Kanvar had first met. Golden ripples flowed over and around the peak—not a single ripple but a whole wave of them.

Kanvar gasped, and Dharanidhar backbeat his wings to stop his forward momentum. A host of men rode the ripples. Kanvar gasped as his mind took in the immensity of the force headed toward him. Nagas and gold dragons—one dozen, two, four dozen, more.

Dharanidhar sucked in a breath, stoking his fires, but he and Kanvar were outnumbered. There would be no fighting these Nagas.

Well, we could fight, Kanvar said, *but we won't win.*

I don't see why that should stop us, Dharanidhar said.

Kanvar. Devaj's mind unveiled itself suddenly, and Khalid's voice spoke from it. *What a surprise finding you here. I thought you'd have joined the force bent on murdering your father.*

I was forbidden to help, but I blame you for the death of my father, not the humans. You vile murderer. You tricked Rajahansa and left him to die. If Khalid thought Kanvar's father was dead, Kanvar figured it best to let him believe the notion. At least it might buy his father time to get to safety.

Khalid laughed. *I don't care whom you blame.*

A shout went up from the Nagas as they caught sight of Kanvar and Dharanidhar. Dharanidhar kept himself in place in the air.

Who are these other Nagas? Kanvar asked Devaj, though he could not feel his brother beyond Khalid's hold on him.

These are my loyal Naga Guardsmen, Khalid said, *led by Theoderic, Lord of Navgarod, come from the Eastern World to restore me to my throne at Stonefountain.*

Dharanidhar whispered to Kanvar, *we'll never have the strength to break Khalid's hold on Devaj if all these Nagas back his mind.*

Kanvar agreed, but continued to talk to Khalid as the Nagas and dragons swept toward them. He had to at least try to find some way to reach his brother's mind. *You've warned them about the singing stones, I suppose.*

Khalid laughed again. *To you, they are stones. To me, they are people. I am the fountain. They are part of me. I know every voice, every tortured cry for help. Each soul of them as if they were my own. I do not fear the singing stones; they will obey my commands.*

Dharanidhar let out a roar and a spray of hot fire, but his fierce anger did not stop the Nagas from flying up around him. They carried loaded crossbows and hemmed Dharanidhar in above, below, and around. Three Great Gold dragons came up in front of him. Their wings rippled as they beat the air to stay afloat. Devaj sat in the center, looking older and more regal than Kanvar had ever seen him. His bearing was that of a king, but his eyes were cold and a sneer twisted his face as he looked on Kanvar.

To his right, rode Lord Theodoric, looking very much like Kanvar's father in flowing golden robes and a circlet of gold on his brow.

On Devaj's left, flew another Naga. Kanvar sensed from his mind that his name was Vitra. He wore a golden vest over a white silk shirt. His golden hair was tied back with a diamond-studded leather thong. His eyes were filled with revulsion as he looked upon Kanvar. The thoughts *abomination, cripple, rogue,* and *traitor* sprang from his mind.

Lord Theodoric lifted a hand in greeting. *Kanvar, my sincerest condolences for the death of your father. As soon as I saw in Kumar Raza's mind that he was in danger, I gathered my men and flew here at all haste. What cruel fate that we should arrive only moments too late to save him.*

Kanvar felt sincerity from Lord Theodoric. He was indeed shattered by the perceived death of the king, but had steeled himself to ultimate loyalty in defense of Devaj who had rightfully replaced his father as ruler of Stonefountain. And if Theodoric was sincere, perhaps Khalid had not gained control of him yet. There may still be a chance to save Devaj.

"My Lord," Kanvar spoke aloud, lowering his crossbow.

"Do not let him speak!" Khalid forced Devaj to shout. "Bind his mind, bind his tongue. He is a traitor. It is he who led the blue dragons and dragon hunters to the palace to kill the king. Kanvar is a murderer and usurper. He seeks the throne for himself."

"No." Kanvar tried to protest further, to explain, but the full force of Theodoric's, Vitra's, and dozens of other Naga minds slammed into his, binding his mind, binding his body, binding his tongue. His crossbow fell from his hand and spun away toward the ground.

Lord Theodoric's dragon flashed a spray of joy breath in Kanvar's and Dharanidhar's faces. Kanvar's mind went fuzzy, and a sense of bliss settled over him as Dharanidhar sank down onto the shelf of rock in the very spot he had crashed when first blinded.

Kanvar felt no pain as Vitra's dragon tore him from his saddle on Dharanidhar's neck and dropped him to the

ground. He felt no fear as Vitra dismounted and unsheathed his sword to execute him. In fact, the whole
situation seemed funny all of a sudden. He giggled as Vitra
swung his sword toward Kanvar's neck.

"Stop," Devaj ordered.

Vitra hesitated. "Why? He's an abomination," Vitra
said with venom in his voice. "He should have been killed
at birth. Your father let him live, and you see what has
come of it, betrayal and murder. You can't possibly mean
to spare him."

"Oh, I have no intention of sparing him. I just don't
want him to die all happy like this. You should not have
sprayed him with joy breath. I want him to feel every pain
my father felt in death, every sword strike, every crossbow
bolt. I was connected with the mind of my father's dragon
when he went down beneath the onslaught. I know what
he felt, and I want Kanvar to feel the same."

Kanvar grinned. What a lovely day it was. What a
beautiful, beautiful day.

"Bind him," Devaj ordered. "Tie his hands, gag him,
shield his mind. Any man who tries to speak with him will
join him in execution. Lord Theodoric, your dragon will
bring him with us. Choose five of your best men to
accompany me. Captain Vitra, you and the rest of your
men will stay here. Make sure the blue dragons do not
follow us. When the singing stones fall silent, take control
of this ragged, filthy human army and bring them to

Stonefountain. They will help us rebuild our home." Devaj tore the sword belt from around Kanvar's waist and claimed his father's powerful sword.

Kanvar hummed to himself while Vitra came to terms with how to bind Kanvar's stumpy left arm as well as his right one and forced a gag into his mouth.

"Wheeee," Kanvar said through the muffled gag as Lord Theodoric's dragon snatched him up in his foreclaw and launched into the air.

An hour later Kanvar didn't feel so good. Flying clutched in the dragon's claw, his stomach churned. The ropes that held his arms pinned at his sides rubbed and burned against his skin with each beat of the dragon's wings and cut off his blood circulation. The gag tasted of sour metal polish that Vitra must have been using on his sword. Kanvar's mind was wrapped away so tightly by Theodoric's that he could barely feel Dharanidhar left behind helpless and blind on the mountainside. The shields suffocated Kanvar's thoughts, giving him the sensation of being buried alive beneath churning waves, and the gag in his mouth compounded the feeling. He screamed, choked, and screamed again, but no one heard him. The wind whipped his hair into his eyes, blinding him, and they flew on and on across the ocean, wind and water and ocean spray drowning him, and he was helpless, helpless . . . his greatest fear. There had to be something he could do, some way to fight, some way to break free. The sun climbed up the sky and crawled down the other side.

He thrashed and screamed. *It's not Devaj. It's not Devaj. Don't listen to him. It's not Devaj. Someone else is controlling his mind. If you want to serve the king, you must help me free him. Please, Theodoric, Devaj's mind is a prisoner. You must help me free him. Don't let him go to Stonefountain. Stop this, stop now, if you have any loyalty to the true king!*

His screams went blocked and unheard. His thrashing only caused the dragon to curl the hand that held him, so sharp claws pressed into his back, piercing his armor and drawing blood.

Dusk had fallen with only a golden sunset in the sky when the dragons swept over Daro. People in the streets below screamed and pointed at the now visible dragons and their Naga riders. Somewhere one lone singing stone came out of its box, probably in the hands of some aging dragon hunter too old to go to Kundiland with the army. A single crossbow bolt launched into the air, but came no-where near the high-flying dragons. Daro was not Khalid's target, not yet.

Then the city vanished away and the savannas stretch-ed out below. The gold dragons slowed as the sun slid behind the horizon.

"No, keep flying," Devaj called. "Stonefountain is close."

Theodoric's dragon winged up beside the smaller Elka-tran. "Your Majesty. My men have been flying since before dawn yesterday with only a short break on the coast of Kundiland when we met you. The dragons must rest and eat. There is no danger here, and there are herds of wild animals below for food. Would it not be better to reach Stonefountain in daylight? There is nothing we can do there tonight anyway."

Kanvar tensed. Theodoric's reasoning was sound, but Khalid was unpredictable. In the moments of silence that followed, Kanvar could hear the trihorn dragons of the Varnan grasslands, bleating below.

"Very well," Devaj said. His voice carried a hint of Devaj's gentle lilt rather than Khalid's harshness. "Of course, your dragons and men must rest."

Devaj, Kanvar tried to call to his brother, but Khalid slapped his mind with a stunning blow that silenced him.

The gold dragons swooped from the sky. Theodoric's dragon dropped Kanvar on the ground and settled down next to him. Kanvar lay where he was dropped, held by Theodoric's mind as well as the ropes that bound him.

"Set camp," Theodoric ordered the five Nagas who had come with him. "Phyric, gather dried grass and bushes and light a fire. Jesson and Unenong, fetch some water from the water hole over there. Weston, you and Bendyn hunt us some dinner. I'll keep watch over the prisoner. Your Majesty, what can I do to make you comfortable?"

Devaj laughed softly, again sounding much like Kanvar's brother. Again, Kanvar reached out to him, only to be blocked by Theodoric's shields and lashed by Khalid.

"I need nothing from you, Theodoric, unless you can call the sunlight back for a few more hours. I had truly hoped to reach Stonefountain this day."

"I'm sorry, Your Majesty."

While Theodoric was focused on his men and Devaj, Kanvar broke his mind free enough to struggle to his feet. It would be so much easier to just stop fighting Khalid, but he couldn't do that.

My Lord, Kanvar said quickly. *I know you can hear me, because it is you holding the shield around my mind. You must listen. Devaj is not himself. Another Naga has taken control of him. If you have any love for your king, then please, let me explain.*

Devaj elbowed Kanvar across the face, knocking him back to the ground. "Silence, beast. You'll get your execution soon enough. I want you to witness my ascension to the throne first. I want you to know that all your treachery has failed before I kill you. Lord Theodoric, if you can't control him, assign one of your men to do it who can."

Lord Theodoric's hold on Kanvar's body tightened.

Devaj strode to the edge of camp and stared into the deepening darkness toward Stonefountain.

"Theodoric, please," Kanvar begged through the gag in his mouth. His words came out only as a muffled groan.

Lord Theodoric drew his sword. "Quiet."

"No. You have to listen." The gag cut into the sides of Kanvar's mouth as he struggled to speak. Theodoric slammed Kanvar in the back of the head with the hilt of his sword, knocking Kanvar unconscious. Kanvar woke later, deep in the night when the fire had fallen to a scattering of red embers and the scent of roasted trihorn had faded nearly to nothing. Dragons and Nagas slept beneath the open stars. Kanvar lay on his side, his feet were bound now as well as his arms. They would not risk him running off while they slept. Someone moved at his back. So, not everyone asleep then. The gag in his mouth tightened for a moment as someone worked the knots loose, then fell away. Kanvar drew in a breath of fresh air, letting it fill his lungs, grateful to be able to breathe freely again. He swallowed and tried to speak, but a hand pressed against his mouth.

Don't speak. Don't say anything to me, Lord Theodoric whispered into his mind. *I don't relish being executed with you. Just be silent, be still. I have some water for you.*

Theodoric helped him sit and pressed a tin cup to his lips. The water inside was hot and muddy, but he appreciated it. His mouth had grown so dry and swollen.

Thank you, Kanvar said.

Silence.

Kanvar stilled his mind as Theodoric retied the gag. Theodoric had risked much just to show him a tiny bit of courtesy. Kanvar did not want to get him in trouble, and yet, he somehow had to communicate the truth of the situation to Theodoric.

Theodoric's mind tightened around his, cutting off any communication between the two of them. Kanvar groaned and rolled onto his stomach so his right hand, which was bound tightly to his side, pressed against the ground. He could not speak with mind or mouth. That left only one option. Carefully he scratched his fingers in the dirt and waited for morning.

Khalid forced Devaj up early. Kanvar stayed on his stomach, covering his work as dragons and Nagas roused themselves and ate a cold breakfast. No one spoke to him. Theodoric's men glanced at him once in a while with looks of disgust. His crippled body was an abomination to them. No matter, he'd grown up with stares like that in Daro. He lay still and silent, compliant to his captors. And waited.

At last, the Nagas mounted their dragons, and Theodoric's dragon lifted Kanvar from the ground. Devaj was already astride his dragon, gazing eastward toward the lone mountain that rose up on the horizon. Theodoric stared down at Kanvar as his dragon lifted him in the air, revealing the writing in the dirt beneath.

Amar lives.
Khalid's spirit controls Devaj.

Theodoric's dragon snorted and tore at the ground with his other foreclaw, obliterating the message. Theodoric said nothing. His face showed no sign he had read the words. Kanvar's heart fell. What more could he do? He had hoped Theodoric was the type of man who would detest Khalid rather than willingly serve him. If he had seen into Kumar Raza's mind, surely he would know Amar, the true, living king, was nothing like Khalid the tyrant.

With a lurch, Kanvar was airborne again.

Chapter Three

Amar groaned and stretched. He lay on a mossy bed in a chamber of Vasanti's lair where she had deposited him after arriving. He'd slept, unable to do anything else until the paralysis from her poison wore off. She'd been apologetic about that, but he'd assured her he understood it was the only way she could get him out of the palace.

Bensharie lay curled up on the floor beside him. There was no way a full grown Great Gold dragon could have fit through the entrance to Vasanti's lair, but Bensharie was just a child. The chamber was dark, except for an oil lamp that burned on the shelf. It would be morning in Daro by now, but the sun was still a few hours away from rising in

Kundiland. Amar shuddered. Dharanidhar's message had been dire when the joy breath had worn off. Kanvar had been taken by an army of Nagas. Dharanidhar had urged the blue dragon pride to go after them, but Khalid had left the main body of the Nagas behind to guard his back. They had fought, and the blue dragons already tired from the battle at the palace, were driven back by the Nagas and their crossbows. Still, there was some hope. Anilon and a few of the blues had broken through and headed for Stonefountain.

Amar tried to stand, but his legs refused to hold him as of yet. He went to his knees and reached out to Bensharie. Scars marred the young dragon's plates. So many scars. Bensharie had felt the pain of the dragon hunter's attack on Rajahansa the moment he'd drunk the blood from the decanter Tana had thrown to him. So many wounds. So much pain for one so young. Tears stung Amar's eyes.

I knew it would hurt. Bensharie's stone glowed as he spoke. His eyes were still closed. Amar had thought he was still asleep, but it seemed he was awake. *I saw what it did to Silverwave when we killed the red dragon.*

"Yes, but Kumar Raza killed the red dragon swiftly. You could not have known Qadim would stretch Rajahansa's death out so cruelly." Amar rubbed his hand along Bensharie's scarred plates. Bensharie's warmth seeped into his hand and spread up his arm to warm his whole body. Their link was deep now, and Bensharie's devotion to him wrapped around his heart, powerful and strange after Amar's long internal battle with Rajahansa. Amar had not dared to think he would ever feel whole again.

Bensharie purred in contentment. *A few minutes of pain to pay for a whole lifetime with you, that's a price I'd willingly pay. Do you think Kanvar is all right?*

Amar groaned and leaned his forehead against Bensharie's chest. "My sons, I've lost both my sons to Khalid. How can I face that? How can I go on living, knowing I failed them so completely?"

Both Devaj and Kanvar were last seen alive, and where there is life there is hope, Your Majesty.

"Amar, for goodness sake, call me Amar. We are bound to each other. You are a king now as well. Use my name now; we are equals."

You are a good deal older than I am.

"And you are a good deal braver and more heroic than I am." Amar hugged Bensharie's neck and sat back. "Oh, Bensharie, what do we do now?"

Bensharie opened his eyes, lifted his head, and ruffled his wings. *I only know the things I've read, but it seems to me that we should move quickly to gather our forces and find a way to counter Khalid. We do not have to fight him alone. Tana and Vasanti are with us, and Kumar Raza will surely take our side.*

Youthful hope spread from Bensharie's mind into Amar's, though Amar's natural defenses resisted it. He'd given up all hope when he'd traded his life to Rajahansa for

Aadi's. "We don't know where Kumar Raza is, and he is only one man."

He is the Great Dragon Hunter, and his brother is with him. Rajan, a Naga so powerful and cunning he nearly took control of the human world all on his own.

Amar let out a bitter laugh. Bensharie was so vibrant and full of life, so sure that evil could be conquered. Amar had felt that way once, but he was old now and had seen too much of the world to believe that things could end happily.

Then I will be young for both of us. Come on. Let's get above the canopy and fly in search of Kumar Raza. Nothing can stop him. He defeated the Maran army in Darvat and slew a Great Red volcanic dragon. Perhaps you and I can't make a difference in saving Devaj, Kanvar, and the world from Khalid, but I have no doubt Kumar Raza can. Bensharie lowered his body so Amar could climb on his back.

Amar took a deep breath and slid into place. He ducked low against Bensharie's neck as Bensharie slid out of Vasanti's lair. Outside, the jungle smelled of damp earth and greenery. The frogs and insects filled the air with song, unaware of the rising evil that threatened to smother the world.

Dead land and crumbling buildings flashed by beneath Kanvar as Theodoric's dragon carried him across the once great city and up to the ruins of the palace on the side of the mountain. Kanvar did not relish returning to this place. He'd visited it once with Kumar Raza and never wanted to return.

Devaj and Elkatran landed in the crumbling chamber where the water ran forth out of the mountain and then fell down the cliff face in a white spray. From his previous visit, Kanvar knew there was a hall that had been opened up by dragon hunters searching for singing stones. It led back into the cavern where Stonefountain bubbled up. But when Theodoric's dragon landed beside Elkatran, Kanvar saw that the hall had collapsed, forming an impassible pile of rubble. The water still jetted forth through its own opening, a conduit that led out from the rubble.

Devaj pointed to the wall of fallen stone. "There it is, Theodoric, Stonefountain. We just have to dig our way into it. Have your men and dragons get to work immediately. Leave the prisoner with me. He and I are going to have a little talk before the end."

"Yes, Your Majesty," Theodoric said. His dragon dropped Kanvar on the rough stone and set to work tearing away the rubble with the other dragons.

Devaj dismounted and walked over to Kanvar who lay on his stomach. It was Devaj's voice that spoke, but the words were all Khalid's. "Well now, abomination." He kicked Kanvar in the side, rolling him over so he could stare down into Kanvar's face. "Last time we were here, you tried to block me from Devaj's mind. Fool, as if your power were even a hundredth as strong as mine."

You have no real power, Kanvar said with his mind since the gag still bound his tongue. *You are nothing but an insubstantial spirit. Your time is over, and this world is nothing like it was when you lived.*

Devaj shook his head. "This world is weak and ripe for the taking."

You will never rule completely, not while there is even one Naga left to stand against you. Kanvar willed away the pain of the ropes that bit into him and the bitter taste of the gag in his mouth.

"And what Naga is that? You?" Devaj kicked him again. "Or perhaps you think your little girlfriend can fight me." Khalid laughed. "Of her own free will she bonded with a green dragon, grounding herself to the jungle. She is no threat to me, though she is very beautiful. Had she bonded with a gold dragon, I might have taken her for myself. She would have been queen of the world. But I'll not have her now for anything beyond a slave in my house."

Kanvar groaned in pain. *Khalid, this is madness. The humans are too strong, the singing stones too many. You will never rule this world. Go back to the fountain, leave my brother alone.*

Stone crunched and ground as Lord Theodoric and his men tore apart the mountain to get inside.

"You have no vision, Kanvar, and no understanding. That is why I haven't killed you yet. I want you to see the full extent of my power before I kill you. I want you to catch a vision of the grandeur of the world as it once was and will be again." Khalid forced Devaj to circle Kanvar like a raptor eyeing its prey.

Kanvar took a deep breath and steeled himself for one last struggle, then he stabbed his thoughts past Khalid, trying to reach his brother's mind. He broke through and found his brother battered and pinned to the back of his own consciousness. *Devaj.* Kanvar reached out to him. *Join me, we can fight Khalid together. We can beat him.*

Devaj stumbled forward and locked minds with Kanvar. Together they gathered their strength to fight Khalid.

Kanvar felt a hot slice of fire across his throat and realized that Khalid had drawn the sword and swept it up against Kanvar's neck. The sharp edge cut into his flesh.

Back in your corner, Princeling, Khalid told Devaj, or *I'll kill your brother right now.*

Devaj let out a cry of despair, broke away from Kanvar, slipped back, and was lost behind Khalid's rage.

Kanvar held his breath. A single flick of Devaj's wrist would end Kanvar's life.

Theodoric's dragon landed beside Elkatran.

"We're almost through, Your Majesty," Theodoric said. "We can hear the scream from the fountain and have lost communication with our dragons while we're near it." His face was pale, and Kanvar wondered if this was the first time Lord Theodoric had heard the cry of the singing stones. No single singing stone could match the volume and intensity of the broken fountain itself.

Khalid swung the sword away from Kanvar's neck and sheathed it. "Good work. Bring him." He pointed to Kanvar. "As soon as the fountain is breached, have your men pull back and give us cover. What I have to do will take some time, but I'm certain you will be pleased with the outcome."

Khalid forced Devaj to stride into the widening gap toward the fountain. Lord Theodoric dismounted, rubbing his hand along his dragon's jawline as he did. He knelt beside Kanvar and drew his saliva-covered hand across Kanvar's throat. His eyes were hard and his jaw tight as he drew his sword and cut the ropes that bound Kanvar's feet, then jerked Kanvar upright.

Kanvar wobbled, his legs too numb to hold him up, but Theodoric caught him from behind and put his own sword to Kanvar's neck while holding him in place.

"Don't try anything foolish," Theodoric said. "Do not speak to me." Theodoric's mind blocked Kanvar's.

Kanvar laughed. A quick swipe of Theodoric's sword would end his life less painfully than anything Khalid had planned.

"Don't even think about it." Theodoric eased his sword away and shook him. "You'll die when the king says you die, and not before. Now move." He forced Kanvar down the cleared path toward the fountain.

Walking was never quick or easy for Kanvar, and Theodoric grew more and more impatient with every limping step Kanvar took. The dragons had cleared a wide swath, unlike the narrow hall that had led to the fountain before. By the time Kanvar and Lord Theodoric passed down it, Theodoric's men had opened a dragon-sized hole into the fountain chamber. The scream of the shattered fountain stopped Theodoric in his tracks. Theodoric gasped and his hand shook so he nearly dropped the sword. Kanvar blanked his own mind to try to ward off the pain.

Close at Kanvar's back, Theodoric's breathing turned ragged. "Get back," he called to his men. "Away from the fountain. Keep guard. Don't let anything interfere."

The other five dragons and Nagas peeled away and retreated to a distance beyond the screaming wail. Devaj strode forward, seemingly unaffected by the broken song of their ancestors. "Come." He motioned Theodoric into the chamber. "You'll want to see this. You will both witness this day, a day most blessed and joyous."

Theodoric forced Kanvar forward into the chamber, but tremors shook Theodoric's body at each step closer to the wounded fountain. Kanvar's mind reeled at the high-pitch wails and discordant voices. Surely there was no greater clamor of torment ever to rise to the sky. It pierced Kanvar, cutting to the marrow of his bones and shredding his heart.

Lord Theodoric dropped his sword. His hold on Kanvar's mind vanished in the blast of screams from the fountain.

Khalid walked Devaj straight to the fountain and set a foot up on the lip.

"No!" Kanvar screamed through the gag and flung himself forward. His shoulder hit Devaj in the chest and slammed him to the ground with Kanvar on top of him. Though Kanvar's hands were tied, he wrestled and writhed to keep Devaj pinned. But Devaj was stronger than he was and unbound. Devaj threw Kanvar off, jumped to his feet, and pressed his foot down against Kanvar's chest.

Khalid laughed. "You will not stop me from taking your brother today and doing more. So much more."

Khalid twisted away from Kanvar, jumped up onto the lip of the fountain, and splashed down into the water. The fountain's spray rained around Devaj's body as Khalid's spirit rose like a glowing tongue of fire and twisted itself into Devaj. Roaring in triumph, Khalid cupped his hands together and lifted them over his head. His eyes glowed with a golden fire. The discordant voices of the fountain rose in pitch. At the height of their scream, Akshara's singing stone appeared between Khalid's fingers, summoned from the chain around Anilon's neck.

Kanvar rolled to his knees in shock. The Nagas could not use their powers in the presence of the singing stones, but Khalid stood in the center of the maelstrom of screams and summoned the stone. How? A cold shiver of realization knifed through Kanvar's bones. The spirit link. It had been strong enough Karishi could call to Raahi's mind a half a world away even while in the presence of General Samdrasen's singing stone. To summon something, a Naga had to be attuned to it, to know it so well it became like a part of them. Khalid knew the fountain, he had spent a thousand years trapped with the remaining spirits inside it.

Khalid lowered Akshara's singing stone into the water, and a dozen spirits flashed out of it with a sigh and went to their rest.

No. Kanvar got to his feet shakily as Khalid summoned more singing stones to him—calling them from around people's necks, from pouches, pockets, and storerooms, summoning them even from the iron boxes that held them. The spirit link Khalid had with the stones was more powerful than any other thing.

One-by-one, bit-by-bit, the fountain healed and its dissonant scream formed into a song. Kanvar told himself to move, to rush forward and stop Khalid, but he found he had no strength to do it, no resolve. It felt right to him, what Khalid was doing, healing the fountain. Restoring the tormented souls to their rest.

A few feet away from Kanvar, tears streamed down Lord Theodoric's face.

The chorus from the fountain rose in a soul-shaking song of triumph, and swept Kanvar's spirit up with it. This was perfection. This was power. This was beauty and joy more sublime than Kanvar's mortal frame could endure. He fell to his knees and wept as Khalid continued his relentless summoning of the singing stones back to their home.

Chapter Four

Still crying, his eyes fixed on Khalid in the fountain, Lord Theodoric lifted his sword from the ground and stepped over to Kanvar's side. He jerked Kanvar to his feet, and pulled him backward away from the fountain.

No, let me stay, Kanvar pleaded. With the fountain nearly healed, the powers of his mind returned.

Lord Theodoric swept his sword up to Kanvar's throat. "Silence, abomination. You are in the presence of the king."

Khalid looked down, fixing eyes on Kanvar and Theodoric. His smile of triumph glowed in the fire of spirit light from the fountain.

Theodoric pressed against Kanvar's back, and held the sword firmly against his throat. He was still shaking, but now instead of using his power to bind Kanvar's mind away from his own, he wrapped a shield around both their minds and let them come together, with his in complete control of Kanvar's. But Theodoric's mind was not cruel and punishing like Khalid's. It was soft and careful. Theodoric opened up a single memory, clear and precise, to Kanvar.

He stood in His Ladyship's chambers while she lay on the bed surrounded by her ladies-in-waiting and attended by the most accomplished midwife in Aesir. Sweat slicked her face as she cried out in the pain of labor. This was her fifth child, and Theodoric prayed to the fountain, *please, please let it be whole.* He'd lost one already, and he could not bear to lose another.

He waited, jaw set, fists clenched on his sword hilt, unable to do anything until the fragile bundle came into the world. The midwife cut the cord and lifted the infant away from its mother. Theodoric took a step toward her. The midwife turned with the child to Theodoric, but her eyes were hard, and she shook her head.

"No!" Theodoric's wife screamed as he took the deformed little boy into his hands. His stomach turned to lead, as the ladies-in-waiting tried to quiet his wife.

"You know the law," the midwife said to her. The midwife's voice was so cold it made Theodoric shudder as he took the child, still glistening with birth fluid and strode out of the room. The law. The law he'd taken an oath to uphold and obey when he'd accepted the crown from his father. His eyes burned and his hands shook as he hurried out of the palace and down to the wooded area of the gardens by the river. Every Naga in the city expected him to obey the law. He was bound by it on pain of his own death and that of his family. Night had fallen while his wife had labored, but he knew this path without light. Too many times he had traversed it, carrying his own child once before and so many others.

He stopped in front of an ancient tree stump, blackened with more than a thousand years of blood, and laid the baby on the wood. Only a few feet away, the waters of the river gurgled against the bank, waiting to consume deformed flesh. Theodoric's sword glimmered in starlight as he drew it. He looked up. A reluctant moon hid behind a stray cloud, curse it. He waited while the baby let out a feeble cry. He put his hand down on the baby's chest and pinched the tender skin. The infant shrieked good and loud as the moon raised its head from behind its cloudy mask.

Theodoric angled his sword blade so the moonlight flashed off of it toward the far bank of the river. A light flashed back to him from the darkened trees beyond.

He pinched the baby again.

Again it screamed.

He held the infant down with his left hand and swung the sword with his right. A good clean stroke that thumped into the wood loudly enough that anyone in the garden or at the palace windows would hear it. At the same moment the sword hit the wood, his mind silenced the baby's screams. The infant wiggled beneath his hand, waving its deformed limbs.

Theodoric pulled a linen wrap from beneath his shirt and wound it around the child. Then he grabbed a water-tight basket from its hiding place in the bushes and sealed the child inside. Grimacing, he tossed the basket out into the river. The Nagas back at the palace would hear the splash. They would not see the net that silently drew up around the basket and pulled it to the far shore.

Steeling himself, Theodoric returned to the tree stump and sliced his own arm open with the edge of his sword. He let the blood flow freely, on the stump, on his clothes, splashing onto his boots. He flung drops out onto the ground as if they'd splattered there when he wielded the blow that killed the infant. He grew dizzy then and his hand went to the vial of Great dragon saliva in his pocket. The cut burned as it healed over. His wife would never know what happened here, and she'd never forgive him for killing another child.

He cleaned his sword and sheathed it, hating himself for his weakness. Knowing he had not really saved his son from death at all, only bought him a few years of life, hidden away in the countryside. A few short years before the dragon fever took him, and he would die anyway, slowly and cruelly, unable to bond with the gold dragons. He couldn't. No one would risk the chance of crippling a gold dragon as well.

This memory of Theodoric's flashed to Kanvar's mind in a split second, followed by another shorter memory of Theodoric looking into Kumar Raza's mind and realizing that a descendant of the royal line still lived. A king could change the law. Only the king. And Amar had let Kanvar live, and more, Kanvar had bonded with a dragon without passing his deformity on to the dragon. There was hope for Theodoric's son and for the other crippled children already born and those yet to be. Theodoric had come to Kundiland in search of that hope. And now he stood face-to-face with the tyrant who had originally uttered the murderous edicts. If Khalid ruled, all hope would be gone forever.

King Amar is alive, Kanvar said. *I swear to you, he lives.*

My men will never believe unless they see him, even then many would follow Khalid instead. Captain Vitra for sure, and others like him.

Let's get out of here, Kanvar said, *while Khalid is still busy summoning the last of the singing stones.* Part of Kanvar still wanted to stay and revel in the joy of the fountain's rebirth, but Theodoric's memory had shocked him back to the reality of what Khalid would do with that restored power. Kanvar considered for a moment that he should get Theodoric to cut his hands free so he could take up the sword and strike down Khalid. But that would mean killing his brother, and his father had forbid him to do that. While Devaj still lived, there might still be some way to banish Khalid's spirit from his body.

Lord Theodoric slipped his sword into its sheath then slung Kanvar over his shoulders and ran. Kanvar thought about protesting that he could walk on his own, but knew there wasn't time. How many seconds would it take for Khalid to realize what had happened? Half a heartbeat? He'd call on Lord Theodoric's men and their dragons to stop them. Kanvar's crippled body could not move fast enough.

As soon as they cleared the chamber, Theodoric's dragon snatched them up and launched into the air.

Stop them! Khalid's command rang out to Theodoric's men, amplified by the power of the fountain.

The other five men and dragons sprang into the air and gave pursuit. Their minds joined with Khalid's in grappling for power to overcome Theodoric's and Kanvar's minds. Kanvar and Theodoric were outnumbered and overpowered and mentally dragged to a stop.

A chorus of angry roars shook the air, and a flight of Great Blue dragons rose up from hiding behind the walls of a crumbling mansion. Hot dragon fire blew into the faces of the pursuing dragons, momentarily blinding them. Anilon slammed Elkatran to the ground, knocking him unconscious and tearing great gouges in his side.

"Stop!" Weston took control of Anilon's mind and forced him away from Elkatran. The other Nagas did the same for the remaining blue dragons. And Kanvar realized in shock what he should have already known. The chain around Anilon's neck, which once held Akshara's singing stone, was empty. The Great Blue dragons knew they had no defense against the Nagas and yet they had attacked anyway, hoping to take them down before losing control. But the Nagas' focus on the blue dragons freed Lord Theodoric's dragon from their control. He dove away, flying hard and fast, putting distance between himself and the other gold dragons, counting on the fact that they would stay in defense of the unconscious Khalid.

Wait, Kanvar cried. *We have to go back. We can't leave the blue dragons to be captured and enslaved. Go back, they are my pride. I have to save them.*

We are not strong enough on our own, Theodoric's dragon said. *We will only be captured as well, and that will do no one any good.* Despite Kanvar's protests, Theodoric's dragon flew on, away from Stonefountain back toward Kundiland.

Kumar Raza gazed across the gray eastern horizon in search of land. His route around the world had seemed so simple when he looked at the map—just keep sailing east until he reached Kundiland. But time had crawled since they'd left behind the eastern coast of Navgarod. In daytime, the sun had been blistering hot, shining relentlessly down on him, Rajan, Dove, and her little girl, reflecting back off the water into their faces. The small boat that Silverwave pulled them in left little room for stretching or moving about. Nighttime had been the only reprieve from thirst and heat. The stars, glittering like jewels in the sky, had been a silent joy to relish while they lasted. But nighttimes came and went, and still there was no sign of Kundiland. In a moment of crankiness, he'd asked Rajan yesterday if Silverwave was swimming them in circles. Rajan's response had been curt. "She knows what she's doing."

At the moment, Silverwave wasn't swimming at all. She was sleeping. Even serpents had to rest sometimes.

"Another day," Dove said softly behind Kumar. He had been sitting alone in the front of the boat and turned to where Dove and Rajan lay in the back with little Eleanor curled up between them. Dove's eyes were open and she stared up into the sky as if she, too, was reluctant to see the stars fade. Rajan still slept.

"We'll make land today. I'm sure of it," Kumar Raza said. In truth, he wasn't sure, but he wanted to be. They'd run out of food and water the evening before, and he worried for the sake of Dove's child.

Dove sighed.

"Are you regretting coming with us?" Kumar asked.

A smile curled the edges of her lips. "I'm a fisherman's daughter. I like being out on the ocean. I was just thinking I had better get up, untangle these nets, and try to bring something in for breakfast. Raw fish may not be appetizing, but they can keep us alive."

Kumar gagged. "I have eaten far too many raw fish in my lifetime. I prefer to avoid eating more if I can."

"When did you eat raw fish?" Dove's eyes twinkled. Kumar liked her and was glad his brother had found such a sweet woman to fall in love with. Both Dove and Rajan had begged Kumar Raza to perform a wedding ceremony for them right there in the boat, but he'd declined, saying the honor should go to Amar.

"I spent a dozen years in the Great North where frozen raw fish and seal blubber are staples. And I tell you, I do not miss it." Kumar scanned the horizon again as pink dawn tinged the sky. A single ray of golden sunshine rose up into the air.

Rajan's eyes snapped open and he jerked to a sit. "What?"

"Dove and I were just talking about raw fish," Kumar said.

"No. Not that. Sh." Rajan lifted a hand to silence Kumar. "Someone's calling your name. Listen."

Kumar listened for a moment but didn't hear anything except the lap of the waves against the side of the boat. "Silverwave isn't even awake yet. Dove, do you hear anything?" he asked.

She shook her head.

Rajan looked at both of them like they were crazy then

jumped to his feet and started waving his arms. "Here! Here! Over here!"

Kumar trained his gaze in the direction Rajan was looking and saw that what he'd taken for a ray of sunshine was in fact a gold dragon, winging across the sky. At Rajan's shout, it changed course and veered toward them. As it drew closer, Kumar realized the dragon was smaller than anyone might expect flying this far away from the palace.

"Is that Bensharie and Kanvar?" he asked Rajan, excitement welling up in him.

Rajan stopped shouting and dropped his hands to his sides now that the dragon had seen them. "It's Bensharie, but not Kanvar. Something is wrong. Very, very wrong." Rajan scowled.

Kumar squinted, trying to make out the rider on Bensharie's back. It was a man, stripped bare to the waist. His unbound golden hair blew in a tangled mess in the wind. "Who is it?" It would be a few minutes yet before Kumar could make out the face. He opened his mind to try and sense who the arriving Naga was. It could be Devaj, but Elkatran was more than twice as large as Bensharie. Parmver's dragon didn't fly much anymore. Rajahansa and Haidar's and Liander's dragons were giants compared to the small dragon that beat eager wings as it shot toward him.

Kumar! It was Amar's presence that made contact with his mind. Amar said something—he was upset, hurt, frightened. Kumar cursed the fact that he was not a full Naga and could only make out impressions from Amar's mind instead of clear speech, though he had managed to rebuild his bond with his twin brother to the point of speech while they'd crossed the ocean together.

"What did he say?" Kumar asked Rajan.

Rajan shook his head. "Nothing that makes any sense. Something about everyone dead and Khalid taking Devaj and Kanvar."

"What?" Kumar's heart raced with fear. Something was indeed wrong.

"I'm sorry. I don't understand what he's trying to say. His thoughts are too jumbled."

Eleanor woke and started to cry. Rajan sat down and drew her onto his lap, comforting her.

Kumar Raza waited with clenched fists as Bensharie crossed the water toward him. As Bensharie drew closer, Kumar was stunned to see scars crisscrossing his golden plates: sword cuts, puncture wounds, and a round spear scar on his chest over his heart. A couple of wing-beats later, Kumar saw that Amar had matching scars. The implications of the sight churned Kumar Raza's stomach. It could only mean that Rajahansa was dead, and Bensharie had taken Amar's bond. What Rajan had said started to sink in. Everyone dead. Devaj and Kanvar taken by Khalid. Had Lord Theodoric and his men not arrived in time to save the palace from the human armies? And what did Khalid have to do with this?

Bensharie circled the boat and then settled into the water beside it. Amar's face was gaunt and pale. The livid white scars on his chest and arms stood out against his sun-bronzed flesh. Bloodstains marred his trousers. There had been a lot of blood spilled.

"Amar." Kumar Raza stood and greeted his friend. "You look horrible. What happened?"

Amar shuddered and swallowed, but didn't speak.

Kumar Raza held out his hand. "Come into the boat and tell me what's happened."

Amar bowed his head. Just breathing seemed to take all of his strength. Bensharie swam to the boat and grabbed onto it, holding it close to his side while Kumar Raza and Rajan helped Amar off the dragon's back. Amar sank to the bottom of the boat and put his head in his hands.

Kumar Raza knelt down beside him and rested a hand on his friend's arm. Little Eleanor crawled up onto Amar's lap and hugged him around the neck. Amar's head jerked up in surprise. He looked at the ragged toddler for a moment then hugged her back. "Dear little one," he said, running his fingers through her dirty blond hair. "Who are you, and how did you come to be sailing with a grouchy old man like Kumar Raza?"

"Da, da," Eleanor said, putting her pudgy hand on Amar's cheek.

"She calls us all that," Rajan said. "Her true father died recently in an earthquake in Aesir."

"Aesir?" Amar asked. At least he was talking now. Leave it to Eleanor to make everyone feel better.

"The capital of Navgarod, the Eastern Country," Kumar Raza said. "We stopped there to help the people ravaged by the earthquake. It is ruled by Nagas. I rallied them and sent them to help you against the human armies."

Amar groaned. "Bad idea. Bad timing. But you could not have known I was counting on those armies to stop Khalid from returning to power."

"I told you sending the Nagas to this side of the world was a bad idea," Rajan said.

"It's not like I had any choice," Kumar Raza said. His body had gone tense, his heart rate increased in the face of danger, ready for a fight though there was nothing out on the ocean he could engage in battle with. "Lord Theodoric helped himself to everything in my mind. It's not like I'm strong enough to shield it from him and the entire Naga Guard. And once Lord Theodoric decided he must come here, there was nothing I could do to stop him."

Amar looked around the boat, seeming to see Rajan for the first time, and Dove beside him. "Forgive me," he said, reaching over and taking Dove's hand. "We have not been introduced. Kumar, please do the honors."

Kumar Raza let out an explosive breath. So like Amar to turn to genteel gallantry even in the face of death and destruction. "Your Majesty. This is my twin brother, Rajan, and his fiancé, Dove. The child on your lap is Dove's daughter, Eleanor. Dove, Rajan, this is His Majesty, King Amar, grandson of King Khalid of Stonefountain."

Rajan stiffened, and Kumar Raza felt his brother's fear. This was the king who would decide if Rajan deserved execution or not. *You have nothing to fear*, Kumar Raza spoke into his brother's mind, *I promise you. Besides, the king is hurt. I think I may need your help to sort out why.*

Red flooded Dove's face. "You, you're the king?" She bowed her head in submission and pulled her hand out of his. "Forgive me, Your Majesty."

"I see nothing to forgive," Amar said, confused.

Dove's voice shook. "I am nothing but a lowly human, a fisherman's daughter. To have looked the king in the face . . . please don't kill me."

Amar shot a startled glance at Kumar Raza. "What?"

It was Rajan who answered before Kumar could think of something useful to explain. "The Nagas of Navgarod did not fall when Stonefountain did. They have ruled that land unhindered for a thousand years, strictly following the laws King Khalid laid down for them."

Moisture rimmed Amar's eyes as he looked from Rajan back to Kumar Raza. "And that is what we can expect from the whole world now. Just before I found you, I got word from Indumauli that all the singing stones are gone, vanished, and I felt an incredible surge of power from Stonefountain. Khalid has succeeded, it seems, in possessing Devaj's body and summoning the singing stones back to

Stonefountain. He has healed the fountain and taken control of the human armies. He'll send Nagas to take control of Maran and Varna next. Kumar, I don't know how to fight him. He's too powerful. And now he has all the Nagas of Navgarod to help him."

Kumar Raza's mind cleared and his fighting senses came into focus. He was a hunter and in the face of danger, his hunting instincts took over. No fear. No confusion. Just strict simple steps. First, learn all you can about the dragon you intend to hunt.

"Amar." He put a firm hand on Amar's shoulder. "I need to know exactly what has happened. Every detail. Leave nothing out. I have a feeling it is important that I get this information as quickly as possible. You have the power to show me everything in your mind. Let's do it."

"No." Amar rubbed his head. "I'm too tired right now. Too hurt and confused. I won't be able to control it."

"Rajan can control it. He and I are linked now like we were when we were young. Let Rajan into your mind, he can sort it out and give the information to me. As soon as I understand what's going on, we can make plans to defeat Khalid."

"You think you can defeat Khalid?" Amar said.

"Of course. I am Kumar Raza, the Great Dragon Hunter," Kumar said, trying to sound reassuring. He did not know how he could defeat Khalid, but he would find a way, whatever it took. "Let Rajan into your mind. I promise, he won't hurt you. He's regained knowledge of the use of his powers. Trust me, he is strong and in control."

You have a lot of faith in me, brother, Rajan said into Kumar Raza's mind.

I know you can do this. Amar needs help. Look at him, even I can sense he can't think straight. He can't even bring himself to talk and tell me what's happened exactly. I don't have the ability to read his mind myself. You can do it. Kumar Raza moved back to let Rajan come up close to Amar.

If he'll let me. Rajan lifting a hand toward Amar's head.

Amar grabbed Rajan's hand, stopping his touch.

Whether he'll let you or not, Kumar Raza told his brother. *If Khalid is involved, Amar might not have the ability left to give you his permission.*

Are you sure?

Yes. Do it.

"Your Majesty," Rajan said aloud. "Let me help you."

"No. I've been through too much. It will hurt you," Amar said.

Rajan laughed, loud and clear. His laugh echoed across the water as the sun slipped up into the sky. "Majesty, I have been the prisoner—mind, body and soul—of a Great Red volcanic dragon for most of my life, and though I don't look it, I am as old as Kumar Raza. Whatever has happened to you can be nothing compared to what I have lived through."

Amar looked at Rajan as if he didn't believe him.

"What? You want to compare scars?" Rajan drew his clothes back to reveal his own bare chest. Sunlight glinted off the purple and red mottled burn scars that covered most of his flesh and turned the four-inch harpoon scar a torrid scarlet.

Amar jolted back against the side of the boat, his face draining of color.

"I'm not going to hurt you," Rajan said softly. "If I have the subtlety to take over the Maran Senate without getting caught, I think I can retrieve your memories without causing you any pain."

Amar swallowed and looked to Kumar Raza for reassurance.

"Amar," Kumar Raza said, keeping his voice soft and even as if coaxing a wild kitrat to him. "Relax. I know I can defeat Khalid, but before I can do that, I need to know what you know. If you can't bring yourself to tell me what has happened out loud, then you must let Rajan see it."

Amar took a deep breath. Bensharie's dragonstone pulsed with light, reassuring Amar. "All right," Amar said. "It's true. I don't want to talk about...about what Khalid did to Rajanhansa...to me. To Parmver, to—" he sucked in a breath, stifling a sob, "—to Aadi. I don't even know if Aadi . . . survived."

"Sh. Don't talk. Just lie back and relax," Rajan said, his words laced with power, a subtle, silky power that wrapped around Amar's mind and gave him a feeling of peace. "Go to sleep, Your Majesty. You will only dream, and no dreams will hurt you."

Amar stilled, his eyes closed, and he fell into an easy sleep.

Kumar Raza let out a breath he'd been holding. "Rajan," he whispered. "I knew you were powerful, but that was frighteningly effective. I'm glad you're on our side. Can you access his memories now?"

"I'm a lot younger than Khalid," Rajan whispered, "so don't count my powers too highly. Yes, I can get what we need from him now. Can you handle it?"

Kumar Raza nodded. "Show me his mind. I need to know everything that has happened."

Chapter Five

Amar woke to the feeling of movement. He was in a little wooden boat, skimming across the ocean waves. Eleanor had curled up under his arm and was resting her face on his chest. Such a darling child. Amar had not been around one so young since Kanvar was little. That seemed like forever ago. Warm sunshine rested on his face, and he had a sense of peace for a moment before his memories jolted him fully awake.

He sat up and realized Kumar Raza and his brother had been arguing with each other. Both fell silent when they saw him awake.

"How . . . was I asleep? How long have I been sleeping?"

"Only a few minutes," Kumar Raza said.

Amar blinked and rubbed his eyes. How could he have fallen asleep knowing that Rajan planned to enter his mind?

His muscles tensed. He should not allow one so young to experience his most horrible memories, despite Rajan's claims to have been through worse. "I'm sorry, Rajan. I just don't think this is a good idea."

"What's a good idea?" Rajan had reclothed, covering his scars.

"My mind. My memories. What's happened," Amar stammered.

Rajan grinned and his sharp white teeth sparkled in the sunlight. Had he filed them to unnatural sharpness? They looked like they could tear as effectively as dragon teeth.

"They can," Rajan said, the smile melting from his face. "But don't worry, Your Majesty. I'm not going to eat you, and Kumar and I have already gathered the information we need from your mind."

"You what?"

"I told you it wouldn't hurt."

Amar stared at Kumar and Rajan for a moment while he searched through his mind for any memory of Rajan entering it. He found none. So this was the Naga that had taken over Maran. It seemed he had learned to use his powers in ways Amar had never dreamed of, but then, Amar had spent his life training his mind to respect the boundaries of other people's thoughts. Eleanor wiggled out from under his arm and crawled across the boat to her mother. Dove kept her head down and would not look Amar in the face. Amar frowned. He would never be the type of king to punish someone for looking him in the eye.

"Why are you frowning," Kumar Raza said. "Rajan didn't hurt you, did he?"

Amar cleared his throat. "No. My mind appears to be untouched. Nice trick that. Rajan, you're a scary man."

"And I'm handsome too." Rajan rubbed the ragged stubble trying to become a beard on his unshaved face.

Kumar grinned at his brother, and Eleanor giggled. Dove's face turned pink.

Amar's face itched from uncut whiskers as well. He couldn't remember when he'd last attended to the niceties of bathing or shaving. His stomach rumbled. Or eating. "What were you arguing about?" he asked the men. It was clear Dove wished only for him to leave her alone. He would honor that.

Rajan crossed his arms over his chest and sat back. He'd lost the argument, it seemed, and wasn't happy about it.

"We were discussing the urgency of our first move," Rajan said. "Since Khalid has stripped the singing stones from the human population, Lord Theodoric and his Nagas can have complete control of the humans. There is nothing to stop them. Even all the Nagas we can rally on our side—you, Rajan, Tana, maybe Karishi, and Aadi, *if* he came down with the dragon fever caused by Rajahansa's action *and* found a dragon to bond with. Denali's too young, but even if we waited until he was old enough to bond with Frost, we are still, all of us together, far outnumbered by the Naga Guard. Power for power, we cannot match them, which means we have to get our hands on some singing stones."

"Impossible," Amar said. "Even if we could get to Stonefountain to steal some more, Khalid would just summon them back again. He has complete control of the singing stones now that he has a body after being a spirit in the fountain for so long."

"Exactly," Kumar Raza said. "The stones from Stonefountain are useless to us. We need singing stones Khalid isn't attuned to. We need gems from the Darvati's Hall of Ancestors. Those will be singing stones too if we harvest them from the walls."

Amar sucked in a breath. He hadn't thought of that. Perhaps there was some hope of stopping Khalid. "If we get the gems from Darvat, he won't be expecting that."

"Wrong," Rajan snapped. "Khalid has control of Devaj, and Devaj knows about the Hall of the Ancestors. He's been there. Rajahansa sent him to Darvat to fetch Karishi, remember? Khalid knows about the stones, and he knows where they are. His first move before anything else will be to take control of Darvat and the Hall."

"Agreed," Kumar Raza said. "He'll move quickly to do that, which is why we must get there first."

"He is closer," Rajan said. "And even if he's distracted for a while with the human armies or by the blue dragons who have gone after him, he won't hesitate to send men to Darvat. We have no way to get to Darvat quickly enough to beat him there. It would take Silverwave forever to circumnavigate Kundiland. Tana's dragon does not fly, and neither does Karishi's. We need time to group our forces and plan a careful and coordinated attack."

"No," Kumar Raza said. "We need to get to the Hall before Khalid's men do. We need to take the stones and get out before they know we've even been there."

Amar rubbed his head. He'd been wrong; clearly the argument between Kumar and Rajan was far from over. "Getting to the Hall of Ancestors is important then?"

"Everything depends on it." Rajan speared Amar with a pointed look. "You and Bensharie are the only ones who have a chance of getting there in time."

"He's the king," Kumar Raza protested. "You can't send the king alone with an infant dragon straight into Khalid's clutches. Amar is our greatest asset. We have to protect him above all else."

I am not an infant, Bensharie protested from where he flew above the boat. *I've faced the Varnan dragon hunters, the Maran army, a Great Red volcanic dragon, and flown the entire distance around the world. A trip to Darvat will be quick and easy after that.*

Amar grinned and leaned back against the side of the boat, reveling in the touch of Bensharie's mind and the courage and sweetness of his heart. *It's all right, Bensharie. You and I will go to Darvat.*

"Why are you smiling? This is serious," Kumar Raza said, raking his fingers through his beard.

"Kumar, dear friend, I can't tell you how happy it makes me watching you carry on like this with your brother whom you thought was dead all these years. After your being alone for so long, and now he's here so alive and so full of fire." For some reason after his short sleep, Amar's heart held more joy and hope than it had minutes before.

Kumar Raza pointed an accusing finger at his brother. "All right, what did you to do him? It feels like he's been hit with joy breath. Our world is ending; Khalid has returned. The human armies are enslaved. What did you do?"

Rajan spread his hands in a gesture of innocence. "All I did was heal over the wound of Rajahansa's passing a bit and ease Amar's shields down so he could deepen his link with young sunshine over there."

Kumar Raza grunted in annoyance.

Amar got to his feet. "Bensharie and I will go to Darvat. You two rally our forces at the new village."

Bensharie flapped down to land by the boat. Silverwave stopped pulling as Bensharie bent his neck down so Amar could climb on his back. On a larger dragon, Amar would have sat at the top of his neck just behind his head, but Bensharie's neck was too small for that yet. Amar fit well enough on his shoulders between his wings.

Father. The faintest whisper reached Amar from Kanvar's mind.

Amar's heart leaped. He'd been unable to reach Kanvar since the Nagas had bound his mind. *Kanvar, you're alive, thank the fountain. Where are you?*

I just escaped Stonefountain with Theodoric's help. A wave of sorrow emanated from Kanvar's mind. *But Devaj is gone, taken by Khalid. I couldn't save him, and he's close to dead now. Anilon attacked Elkatran and almost killed him...came so close, even without Akshara's singing stone—the stones are gone, back to the fountain. But Anilon failed, the Nagas stopped him before the final blow. His actions bought Theodoric and me our freedom, but the blues are enslaved now. Who knows what Khalid will do to them.*

Amar's mind spun. Kanvar had confirmed the worst, which Amar had already figured had happened. But more. Though Amar wished Devaj no harm, if Elkatran was seriously wounded then Khalid was wounded, and that had just bought them some time. And as much as Amar wanted to feel young and free again and fly off to Darvat with Bensharie, Kanvar was closer.

Kanvar, are you still in Varna?

Yes, but we're coming back. Lord Theodoric thinks if you show yourself to his men so they know you're alive then some of them, less then half, but some will join you instead of Khalid. Kanvar's thoughts were clipped, and Amar could feel through their mind link that Kanvar was bound and gagged.

Theodoric hasn't untied you?

There wasn't time. We had to get away. He'll do it soon. I promise.

"What are you waiting for?" Kumar Raza's gruff voice interrupted Amar's conversation with Kanvar.

"Kanvar's free. I'm sending him and Lord Theodoric to Darvat," Amar said.

We're going to Darvat? Why? Kanvar had heard him.

Amar relayed the critical nature of the mission to Darvat.

Kanvar accepted the information but hesitated. *Dharanidhar. He's stuck blind on the mountain. He can't fly. He can't hunt. He has no water. I have to get back to him.*

I'll find a way to help him. I promise. You, go, fly fast. Now link with Theodoric for a moment so I can talk to him.

Kanvar's mind went fuzzy for a moment. Then a new mind joined them. Lord Theodoric's thoughts were guarded. He reached out to speak with Amar hesitantly.

Your Majesty? Forgive me for acting against your wishes. Devaj told me you were dead. I had no choice but to follow his commands. He's your heir. I-I'm sorry. I did not know about Khalid until too late.

What happened is not your fault, Amar reassured him. *Khalid has manipulated all of us to achieve his ends. We have only one good chance to stop him. You must fly Kanvar to Darvat. Obey whatever he tells you as if the orders came from me. Do you understand?*

Yes, Your Majesty.

And for goodness sake, untie him.

Shame flashed back through the link. *Yes, Your Majesty. Of Course. Forgive me.*

Lord Theodoric, you have nothing to be ashamed of. You saved my son. I welcome you to my service. I can't begin to tell you how much it means to me. Even if you are the only Naga from Navgarod to take a stand with me against Khalid, I welcome it. Amar conveyed a feeling of appreciation and reassurance to Theodoric though he did not know why Theodoric had taken his side.

Majesty, you are the king. I have given my oath to serve you.

Thank you. Now fly quickly. If Kanvar does not succeed at this, the odds of us ever defeating Khalid are much reduced. Amar pulled his mind back from Theodoric and Kanvar's. His head swam and a headache stabbed across his forehead. Bensharie was not nearly as old and powerful as Rajahansa had been. Amar would have to remember that his powers were slightly lessened now and not push so hard he knocked both of them out.

Bensharie groaned and rubbed his head.

"Sorry, Bensharie." He patted Bensharie and urged him into the air, telling Silverwave to follow them to the bay where the new village was being built.

Lord Theodoric's dragon set Kanvar and Theodoric down next to the small oasis and settled into sand beside them.

Quickly, Kanvar said. *I don't know how much time we have before they come after us.*

Theodoric drew his sword and cut the ropes that held Kanvar's arms bound against his sides. Then he untied the gag and pulled it from Kanvar's mouth. Kanvar gasped and pushed himself up with his good arm. Pin pricks spread up it as full blood flow returned. He got to his feet and stumbled over to the oasis to quench his parched and swollen mouth. A flock of silver-winged birds flew up, filling the air with their shrill cries as he approached the water. The water was warm and clear. He took a long drink, then washed the dust from his face and wet down his hair.

Theodoric scooped a handful of water for himself and turned to stare back the way they'd come. "I'm sorry about your pride; those blue dragons, I never thought they'd do something like that. Surely they knew they'd be captured."

"It was worth it to them for the chance they might kill Khalid. In any case, they have bought our freedom and given us time to get to Darvat ahead of the Naga Guard. Let's not waste it." Kanvar's hand went to the crossbow harness on his back and came up empty. He'd lost the crossbow his grandfather had made for him. Growling under his breath he dropped his hand to his side. It again closed on empty air. And Khalid had the king's sword.

As soon as Theodoric's dragon finished drinking, he lowered his head so Theodoric could climb up on his neck. Theodoric held out his hand to Kanvar. "Ishayu is strong enough we can both ride him. Climb up here in front of me."

Kanvar climbed up on the dragon's neck and winced as the golden plates locked him in place.

"Are you comfortable, Your Highness?" Theodoric asked as Ishayu launched into the air and headed in the direction Kanvar ordered.

"I prefer riding my own dragon," Kanvar said.

"He is far too old for you," Theodoric mused. "It seems strange that you should be bound to such a creature."

Kanvar let out a bitter laugh. "What gold dragon would have taken my bond, fearing he too would be crippled?"

Theodoric tensed behind Kanvar. "None that I know."

"In truth, Bensharie would have done it. I know of no other gold dragon as courageous as he is. I think I could have bonded with Bensharie, and we'd both have been happy. But I'd already bounded with Dharanidhar quite by accident. Did you not learn what happened from my grandfather's mind?"

"I was searching for other things when I read his thoughts."

Kanvar took a deep breath and savored the wind blowing in his face. Ishayu's flight was smooth and fast as he shot north-eastward. "It was an accident. I was holding my father's sword when Dharanidhar snatched me up in his claw. It cut both of us. The blood...we didn't exactly drink it at that time, but it mixed in our wounds. Later we chose to complete the bond more fully, and I don't regret it. Neither does Dharanidhar. We are two of a kind, despite the age difference. My personality is much more fitting a

Great Blue dragon's than a gold's. And truly, no dragon could better take Rajahansa's place for my father than Bensharie."

"How could that happen? How is it your father lives?"

Kanvar kept his eyes on the eastern horizon, hoping for good weather when they reached the ocean. "You've heard the story of Nikeron?"

Lord Theodoric tightened up another notch. "Yes, but it is only a story."

"It worked with Rajan, so I knew it would work for my father. It was the only way to free him from Rajahansa who had turned evil through Khalid's influence. He tortured and chained my father; he had to die."

"The law requires imprisonment for those who would abuse their bond," Theoderic said. "Execution would risk the life of the innocent."

"You don't get it, do you?" Kanvar said, anger welling up inside him. "The old laws are dead, have been for a thousand years. This world is brutal and unforgiving. For a Naga to survive, he must be willing to fight anyone, everyone, to spit life in the face, to roar into the wind and keep roaring until fate tears his voice from him and buries him with the bones of all the other Naga dead."

Theodoric cleared his throat. "You really are a blue dragon."

"I was born crippled," Kanvar said. "Every day of my life has been a fight. Every step I take, a battle. My mother tried to murder me when I was a small child. I escaped and survived on my own for years, hiding what I was, searching for any Great dragon who would take my bond. If I seem ferocious to you, it is because I've had to be. I know that's hard for you to understand, you who have spent your life in castle halls, surrounded by servants to wait on your every whim. But you have left your sheltered world behind and stepped into mine. Now you must learn to fight to survive, or die. You must be willing to kill if that's what it takes to defeat evil and secure freedom for this world."

Theodoric's hand closed around his sword hilt. "So, you'd risk killing your own father? Khalid did not lie when he said you led the dragon hunters to the palace?"

Kanvar's hand clenched into a fist. "That is true, but it was all part of Khalid's twisted plan. He led us to believe that Rajahansa would take my father to Stonefountain so Khalid could possess his body and rise again. My father ordered me to kill him to keep that from happening. None of us realized until too late that the whole brutal play was only a diversion so Khalid could take Devaj."

Kanvar gritted his teeth as he sensed Lord Theodoric working through his own anger and revulsion. At last, Theodoric's hand moved from his sword hilt to clasp Kanvar's arm. "I have been arrogant and blind, judging this world by the perceptions from my own. Forgive me and …be patient. I doubt I can change what and how I am. I have been brought up to despise everything you are, but I think we must work together anyway. In any case, I must do so at your father's direct command."

Kanvar let himself smile. He liked Theodoric. At least the Lord of Navgarod was willing to accept Kanvar for what he was, unlike Rajahansa, Haidar, and Liander.

"How old is your son, the crippled one you showed me?" Kanvar asked.

"He'll be sixteen this year, but I haven't seen him since the night he was born. I do not know where he is or how he fares. He may already be dead from the fever, but I'd like to think that he is alive, and I can save him."

Kanvar shuddered to think of Theodoric's son already burning with the dragon fever. "You have many children?"

"I sent my oldest son, LaShawn, to Stonefountain long ago to seek for news of any survivors. He never returned, and I must assume he is dead. My next child, a daughter, was born crippled. I have no hope that she yet lives. I have two daughters who have grown to adulthood and married. Then the little boy you saw and two other children. The younger of the two, the sweetest little girl ever born to this world, died in an earthquake that shook Aesir not long ago. I left her brother, Shaunty, in his mother's care." Theodoric fell silent, and Kanvar could think of nothing else to say.

Of Theodoric's seven children, only three had survived for sure. Kanvar thought of Tana and wondered if he and she might ever have children. It did not seem likely.

Now that Khalid had returned, all Kanvar could see ahead of him was fighting. And what of it? In the end, it was his own older brother he was fighting. The brother whose life he'd risked everything to save. The sight of Devaj in the fountain, his eyes glowing with Khalid's power, would haunt Kanvar forever.

The singing stones from the Hall of Raahi's Ancestors might turn the tide of battle, freeing General Chandran's armies to engage the Naga Guard, but the only final solution Kanvar could see was Devaj's death. It made his stomach churn and bile rise to the back of his throat. And even if Devaj did die and Khalid return to the fountain, what was to keep him from luring some other Naga with the promise of power to free him once more. All fighting was in vain unless Kanvar could think of a way to rid the world of Khalid forever.

Chapter Six

Dharanidhar stood motionless on the side of the mountain where Lord Theodoric and the Naga Guard had left him after hitting him with the joy breath the day before. This was the second time in his life he'd been stranded blind on this ledge. The first time he'd been angry and been driven by a thirst for revenge so strong he had taken flight into his now darkened world, following the one pinpoint of light in his mind—Kanvar. He had been able to feel him as he followed the river down to the village and was taken from there to the golden palace. He'd hungered for Kanvar's blood, wishing to tear him into oblivion. That fool human boy who had blinded him with a single sword strike. That defiant crippled boy who had destroyed Dharanidhar's life and offered it back to him whole and more wondrous than he could have imagined. Dharanidhar rumbled and dug his claws into the ground where he stood, feeling the rock chip and soil bunch in his grasp.

This time Kanvar had been carried far away, and though freed now was flying even farther. Dharanidhar's thoughts and hopes winged with him. *Fly, boy, fly. Akshara left the defense of the world in our hands.*

We will not fail. But Dhar, you're hungry and thirsty. You need more medicine.

I will survive. Dharanidhar broke his thoughts off from Kanvar and let them focus on the jungle below him. His physical eyes could not see, but his bond with Kanvar had gifted him with mental sight instead. Sight he had learned to harness while living alone in the cove after being exiled from the blue dragon pride and banished from the palace. He'd gone hungry at times in the cove, true, but he had begun to learn how to feel the world around him, a vivid world full of life and wonder.

A steamy heat rose from the jungle below him, smelling of musty fungus, damp leaves, sweet orchids, and black monkeys. Insects filled their air with a steady buzz, interrupted by the sharp cry of birds. But Dharanidhar's sense of the jungle went beyond sound and smell, he could sense the trees themselves, feel them stretching and growing. The fleeting existence of every bird and bug and frog dwelt upon his consciousness. The black monkeys and lesser dragons were brighter in his mind, more self aware, searching for food, licking their wounds after the battle they'd fought with the humans, trying to shake off the confusion left when Haidar's and Rajahansa's mind control sprang away from them. And blazing bright, as gold as the sun at noon, the minds of the Naga Guardsmen as they secured their hold on the human armies and forced them back down the river to the coast. Dharanidhar kept his mind veiled from them in hopes they'd forgotten about him or discounted him completely after snatching his Naga away from him. Several other Great Blue dragons were already in their power, but most of the pride had been driven back the night before and returned to their nesting grounds after Anilon had broken past the Nagas and set out across the ocean.

In their arrogance, the Nagas discounted Dharanidhar completely. He was a blind, crippled, old dragon past his prime and useless for anything.

Useless. Dharanidhar puffed a thin stream of blue fire. I'll show them useless. But he could not fight them. Not yet. He'd have to wait for Kanvar's return. He was not sure if he dared fly with only the sense of his mind. The longer he sat there, the more he'd been able to feel, even to the point that he imagined the rocks had a soul. They did not grow and struggle like the plants and trees. They did not fight for food like the insects and animals. The rocks, the mountains, they did nothing but exist. He could not describe it any other way. But his sense of them was faint, and he still feared he would crash again as he had before.

The simple thoughts of a lesser green serpent crept down the side of the mountain behind him. It had just eaten. Its belly full, it sought the cool safety of its hole.

Dharanidhar swiped the green serpent from the side of the cliff and held its wriggling body tight in his claw. His stomach rumbled and mouth watered. Here was food at last.

The serpent's frightened thoughts skittered through his mind. The creature was not intelligent. It did not think like a Great dragon or human would. Its mind knew only *danger, run, escape.* It looked up at the blue dragon in terror. *Run, run, run.* Its stubby serpent legs wind-milled against Dharanidhar's foreclaw.

Dharanidhar opened his mouth and moved the serpent toward it. He was so hungry.

The serpent panicked and blinked in terror at the blue monstrosity that held it. Big as a mountain. Teeth flashing. Scarred, milky-white orbs where its eyes should be. The clear image of himself from the green serpent's mind shocked Dharanidhar, and he froze with the serpent only inches from his mouth.

You fear me? You think I'm a monster? Dharanidhar said to it.

The green serpent couldn't understand his words any more than if they had been a growl. Its mind was incapable of speech. It knew only sleep, hunt, eat, and mate. And how pleasant it was to soak in the sunshine on the side of the cliff.

But you can see, Dharanidhar said. *You can see me.* Excitement blossomed in his chest. *I can see* me *through your eyes.*

The lesser green serpent continued to pant and squirm in his grip. Its tongue flicked in and out, desperate for escape.

Easy there now, Dharanidhar said, stroking the creature's head and neck. It did not understand his words, but he used his power to dissolve the creature's fear and make it feel that it should trust him. *I'm not going to eat you. Not right now, anyway. Be still. Be still.* He opened his claw and stroked the serpent's stomach until it lay quietly in his hands. *You see, you're safe with me. You and I are going to be friends.*

Dharanidhar had never before purposely used his power on another creature, but it came to him easily now and felt right. Yes, he had affected the serpent's mind, but in a friendly way. He made the serpent like him. He assured it they would be partners. It could trust Dharanidhar. It need not be alone. It need never go hungry. It need fear no other creature as long as it stayed with Dharanidhar.

We are one, you and I.

The serpent willingly accepted Dharanidhar's mind as part of its own, and Dharanidhar looked out at the world through its eyes. He lifted the serpent to his neck. It wrapped itself around him and laid its head down right between Dharanidhar's useless eyes. And he could see the whole world in all its splendid color. He could see the beach where the Nagas loaded the human armies back on their boats. He could see the blue ocean beyond, and when he turned his head, the jungle below, and the mountains behind. His heart leaped with joy. He cared for Kanvar as much as his own life, but he no longer needed his Naga friend to see.

Silently he took flight away from the Naga Guardsmen and their human slaves.

Hugging the tops of the trees, he flew upriver toward the palace. His low flight startled a leatherwing awake, and it broke up into the air. He snatched it from flight and devoured it, offering some to his new friend whom he named Kivi.

Kivi sniffed it and lowered his head. He was not hungry. Later he would share Dharanidhar's meals.

As Dharanidhar winged past the palace, he caught sight of movement in one of the windows. He flinched and dropped lower, hoping to avoid the gaze of any gold dragons. But Kivi lifted his head and craned his neck around to see better. There were humans up there, not dragons. Dharanidhar growled. General Chandran and the dragon hunters. Anilon had dropped them off to do their dirty work and left them there in his mad scramble to try to stop Devaj. They were trapped in the palace they had turned into a death chamber.

Dharanidhar snorted in contempt, figuring he should leave them there to starve and decay away to skeletons. They were enemies of all Nagas. But an annoying thought niggled into his mind. Kanvar was fond of General Chandran. Despite the fact that Chandran had stabbed Kanvar through the gut with his sword, Kanvar still counted Chandran as a friend and ally. In the battle against Khalid, would they not need all the allies they could get?

The dragon hunters' shouts for him to rescue them were fading away behind him when he wheeled around and flew back. His body ached. Without the medicine, every flap of his wings was growing excruciating. He had to get back to the new village where Devaj had taught the villagers how to make the medicine. Strange that, Devaj had been so adamant and urgent that he teach others to make what Dharanidhar needed. Devaj kept saying, "I might not always be here. You must learn this." Had he known Khalid would take him? Had he known and not warned anyone? Had he known but Khalid had prevented him from speaking out, from warning his friends and family? What torture that must have been.

Dharanidhar growled, but did not let out the roar and burst of flame he wanted to. Something like that might draw the Nagas' attention his way. He was far beyond their sight now, but not beyond their minds. He must stay quiet and move like a shadow. He rose up to the window where the dragon hunters waited. They were armed with cross-bows, spears, and swords. Would they attack him? They'd be fools if they did. The only other rescue they could hope for would be into slavery with the Naga Guard.

"Put your weapons away," General Chandran told the dragon hunters.

Dharanidhar opened his jaws a crack and let blue fire spark behind his teeth.

"He'll kill us," one of the younger dragon hunters said.

"No," Chandran said. "We have an alliance with the blue dragons. An agreement."

"Apparently your agreement didn't include getting us back down from here," Qadim said.

"An oversight on my part," Chandran said. "But we could have arranged that if you hadn't been so anxious to kill Tana. She was our ally and you shot at her."

"Too bad I missed," Qadim said. "Stupid green dragon. Since when did Nagas bond with anything besides golds?"

Dharanidhar snapped his jaws closed and let out a low warning growl. He could not stay airborne in one place for much longer. His wings ached too much. This type of flight was the hardest. He dropped below the window and wheeled away.

Chandran cursed. "Put your weapons down and step away from the window so he can land."

Reluctantly, the dragon hunters lowered their weapons and stepped away from the window as Dharanidhar came back around. He swooped in the window and landed on the annoying gold-leafed floor. A groan escaped him as his back legs took the weight of his body. He folded his wings and shook his head. Kivi squealed as Dharanidhar's movements almost dislodged him.

Sorry, little friend. Lie back down. I'll try to remember not to do that again, he reassured him.

Kivi hissed and settled back down on Dharanidhar's forehead.

"Thank you for coming," General Chandran said. "We thought you'd forgotten about us. Will you take us to the beach?"

Dharanidhar growled and shook his head slowly to keep from unsettling Kivi.

"Why not?" Qadim demanded.

Dharanidhar growled and dug his claws into the floor. Trying to talk to humans was useless.

The dragon hunters reached for their swords and crossbows.

Stupid fools. Dharanidhar lumbered past them, heading deeper into the palace, past halls and doorways until he came to a chamber he'd avoided on previous visits. It was usually full of annoying gold dragons scribbling away on parchment, writing who knew what. Well, poetry in Bensharie's case, but the rest of them . . . Dharanidhar did not know or care what they wrote. He grabbed an ink well from the table at the center of the room and a stack of parchments then turned to go back to the humans, but found they'd followed him.

Fine. He slapped a parchment down on the table, dipped a single claw into the inkwell, and wrote. *Khalid tricked us. The battle here was a diversion. He took Devaj to*

Stonefountain and possessed him. The singing stones are gone, and he's summoned a Naga army from a land eastward past the Eastern Isles. Your men are enslaved.

Qadim swore long and loud, using every foul word he knew then cycling back around to use them again a few more times.

"We can't fight an army of Nagas, not without singing stones," General Chandran said. "Where have the stones gone?"

Back to the fountain. Khalid's spirit is linked to them. Inside a living Naga body, he can summon them at will. Dharanidhar flicked the excess ink off his claw, crumpled the parchment, threw it in the air and burned it with an angry breath.

"Then there is no hope," Qadim said. "The world is lost."

"Not while we still have breath to defy him," General Chandran said.

"How can we fight him?" Qadim spat. "He will take our minds and enslave us. We have no chance against his power."

"Perhaps he can control us," General Chandran said, caressing his sword hilt. "But I doubt he can control another Naga so easily."

"What other Naga? That pretty little girl?" Qadim asked. "We've killed all the ones that are any threat to anyone."

Dharanidhar laughed. Raising his head, he let out the torch of blue flame he'd been holding back. He laughed until his deep voice rattled the palace walls. The young dragon hunters stepped back and drew their weapons, ready to duck for cover behind the pillars if Dharanidhar blew fire at them.

Qadim loaded his crossbow. "I've never heard a dragon growl like that before, Chandran. I don't like the sound of it."

Chandran snorted. "He's laughing at you, Qadim." Chandran walked to the table and pushed a clean parchment over in front of Dharanidhar. "How many Nagas are left who will help us fight Khalid? Who are they and how powerful?"

Dharanidhar was beginning to see why Kanvar was so fond of General Chandran. Dhar figured he could trust Chandran, but he did not trust Qadim and the dragon hunters with the truth about all the Nagas. He did not know how much Tana had told them. He snatched up the ink well and threw it against the wall, shattering it and sending ink spraying over the dragon hunters.

"Doesn't look like laughing to me," Qadim said.

"You're pointing a crossbow at him." Chandran walked down to the next station at the table and came back with another ink well. "Forgive me, Your Mightiness. I get the feeling you do not trust us. And we have given you no reason to do so. We are trapped here and at your mercy. Will you fly us down from the palace?"

Where would you have me take you? Dharanidhar wrote.

"Are Khalid's Nagas watching the jungle village?"

I don't think they know about the village. They can't see it from the air. They seem to be focusing their attention on taking the humans with them to Stonefountain. All the Nagas I sensed were gathered at the beach, but I cannot guarantee the village is safe.

The youngest of the dragon hunters, a man with dark brown hair clasped in a leather thong at the back of his neck, dressed in reinforced leather armor that looked battered enough to verify he'd seen plenty of action, set his crossbow on the table and shook his head. "I cannot believe we're having a conversation with a Great Blue dragon. I used to daydream when I was a child that I would get to speak with a Great dragon some day. What is your name, Great One? How is it you have come to help us?"

Qadim glared at the young man.

Dharanidhar blew a wisp of blue fire at Qadim and dipped his claw back in the ink to answer the youth. If more humans were like him, dragons and humans might be friends again one day.

My name is Dharanidhar. I am a descendant of Akshara, and he charged me with his dying breath to defend the freedom of this world. It was the blue dragons who brought Khalid down a thousand years ago, and we will do so again now, with or without your feeble help.

The young dragon hunter rested his hand on his sword and stared up into Dharanidhar's face. "My name is Bitterwood, and I will help you fight Khalid. I don't know how it is that Nagas have crept back into the world, but I have taken an oath to see them all destroyed."

Dharanidhar's anger exploded, hot and out of control. He roared and flung the table across the room. It slammed into two of the pillars, toppling them. Stones from the ceiling crashed down into the room. The dragon hunters raced out of the chamber. Dharanidhar tore down two more pillars and lashed the rubble with his tail. Walls crumbled behind him as he stalked away. Kivi hissed, ducked his head, and closed his eyes.

Dharanidhar's world went black. He hesitated in the hall, calming his breathing, getting his rage under control. He'd been right not to tell the dragon hunters that Kanvar, Amar, and Rajan still lived. All three supposedly dead. The dragon hunters could not be trusted. Dharanidhar felt the hot burn of a crossbow bolt hit his side. Bellowing, he stoked his fire and prepared to finish the hunters.

"No wait!" Chandran's voice cried out. "Do not fire again. I order you to put your weapons away."

"We do not take orders from you," Qadim said.

"You kill this dragon, and we will all die here!" Chandran said.

"He attacked us." Bitterwood's voice cracked with fear.

"He did not attack us," Chandran said. "If he had, we'd all be blackened corpses. He's a blue dragon, boy, and blue dragons are known for their tempers. Something you said upset him. That's all. It does not mean he wants us dead, and we certainly don't want him dead. Just stop and think for a minute."

"I was trying to agree with him," Bitterwood muttered.

Dharanidhar growled, tore the crossbow bolt from his side, and licked the wound closed. He supposed he had overreacted, but he'd been holding the anger and frustration in for so long. *Open your eyes*, he urged Kivi.

Reluctantly, the little green serpent opened his eyes a slit. Chandran stood with his arms spread between Dharanidhar and the other dragon hunters. Of course, he was so small compared to Dharanidhar that he could not possibly have blocked any of the hunter's bolts, but Dharanidhar appreciated the gesture.

"Be quiet," Qadim snapped at Bitterwood. "You should know better than to speak up during a delicate negotiation."

Lifting himself upright, Dharanidhar stepped overtop of General Chandran and the dragon hunters and made his way to the closest chamber with windows. From close by he could smell the stench of a dead gold dragon. Rajahansa. *I will not miss him*, Dharanidhar growled.

At the window, he turned back to face the dragon hunters. He'd left behind any way to communicate with the men. No matter, he was done talking. He snatched three of the men up in one foreclaw, three up in the other. Then he beat his wings to lift himself off the ground and caught up three more in one hind claw and General Chandran in the other. Humid air hit his face as he dove out of the window and curved his wings into a glide, following the river around and down toward the coast.

Dragonbound VII

A hot burn throbbed in his wings and legs by the time he reached the cliff shelf above the village. He'd neither seen nor felt any Nagas or human soldiers. Flapping his pain-filled wings, he hovered above the shelf and let the dragon hunters down. They looked rumpled and disoriented as they tumbled out of his claws. He blew a goodbye lick of fire at the men then turned and flew away with General Chandran still in his grip.

Chapter Seven

Bensharie landed on the white sand of the beach outside the new village. Amar climbed from his back and looked over to the ground the villagers had cleared at the edge of the tree line. The villagers were now constructing the round huts that would be their new home. He doubted building on the ground was as secure as the original village, but building platforms would take time, and the villagers were still in shock at the move. He could feel their surprise and bewilderment as they worked methodically to rebuild their lives, thatching their huts, arranging their belongings, organizing a hunt for food. These were his people. If he could claim any kingdom his to care for it was them, and the arrival of the human armies had endangered their lives and forced them to leave their homes. It was a miracle that Elkantran and Bensharie, both such young dragons, had managed to move so many people so far so quickly. Amar could hardly fathom how they'd done it.

We flew, a lot, Bensharie said. *We carried a lot. We did not sleep. I do not see how Khalid could have been in control of Devaj. I've known Devaj for so long and sensed nothing amiss in his mind as we were working together. He cared only for the safety of the villagers and worried for your welfare.*

Silverwave pushed the boat on shore, and the humans climbed out of it. Kumar Raza scowled at the circle of huts as he walked up beside Amar. "Was it Devaj who picked this spot to build the village?"

Bensharie nodded.

"I don't like it." Rajan carried Eleanor in his arms and held Dove's hand.

"It seems like a beautiful place to me," Dove said. "There is fresh water from that river there, and the bay is calm and perfect for fishing. There is plenty of wood to build homes and cook with. The soil looks fertile enough to plant crops. This place is paradise compared to Aesir."

Sweat slicked Amar's palms. Dove was right, this place was perfect. The only thing wrong with it was that Khalid must have been behind the move.

"We have no way of knowing how much influence Khalid had over Devaj at what time," Kumar Raza said. "The only thing we can be sure of is that Khalid knows where this place is. The question is, will he strike here?"

"I would," Rajan said. "It's the most likely place for his enemies to gather."

"How many enemies do you suppose he thinks he has left?" Kumar asked. "Tana, Karishi, Kanvar. He thinks Amar is dead. I am not a Naga, so he's unlikely to see me as a threat, and he doesn't know about you."

"He'll attack this place. I'm sure of it." Rajan hugged Eleanor tighter to him. "We have to move these people somewhere safe."

"We can't make the villagers move again." Amar started across the sand toward the village. "If you think it will be attacked, then we need to find a way to defend it."

"We can't defend this," Kumar Raza kept pace with him. "It's completely open. There's nothing I can use here. The village is an easy target for gold dragons."

Amar clenched his fists. "Then I suppose Khalid knew exactly what he was doing."

"Precisely," Rajan said. "We must move the villagers deeper into the jungle so the gold dragons can't get down through the trees, or move the villagers up into a mountain somewhere so we can build fortifications, mount ballistae, use narrow tunnels and caves for cover."

Seeing Amar approach, the villagers stopped their work and began to gather. Jabari, the village leader strode out to meet him.

"Kumar." Amar grabbed Kumar Raza's arm and stopped him before Jabari reached them. "We must take this war to Khalid at Stonefountain. It doesn't matter where this village is; without the singing stones these people are defenseless. The Nagas can feel their minds and take control of them here or in the jungle or in the mountains. But this is only a small group of people. Khalid will have no reason to do anything with them if we present a more important target elsewhere."

"Is there a problem, Your Majesty?" Jabari said, bowing. "You look to have gone through some terrible fighting. Are we in danger? I thought the Maran and Varnan armies would never come here."

"I doubt Kanvar will fail to get the singing stones," Kumar Raza said, ignoring Jabari. "But I agree with you. This is not a good place for us to gather our forces and plan an attack on Stonefountain."

"Attack Stonefountain?" Jabari's brow furrowed.

"Come, my old friend," Amar said to Jabari. "I will tell you everything, but let's go somewhere we can sit down. I'm not feeling my best right now." Amar motioned Jabari to the ring of huts. As they approached the crowd, a shrill cry went up and Mani raced out to meet him.

"Amar, Amar." Her cool fingers slid across the scars on his chest and tears sprang into her eyes. "What happened?"

"Mani, it's all right." He took her into his arms to still her shaking, but she would not be so easily reassured.

"You're hurt. Look at you. What did Rajahansa do to you?"

"Rajahansa did nothing. It was the human dragon hunters. They killed him."

Mani looked up into his face. "But you're alive?"

"I'm alive, thanks to Bensharie. And I'm glad to see you safe and alive as well. Can you get me some food and water? I need to rest a moment."

"Of course." Mani gripped his hand and led him through the crowd toward one of the huts. When he looked back, he saw that Kumar Raza was having a happy reunion with his wife, Eska, and son, Denali, while Miki barked a greeting and Frost flapping around them, her dragonstone sparkling white in the sunlight. Amar hoped the ocean breezes were keeping it cool enough for her here.

Kumar Raza and his family followed Amar and Mani, and a few minutes later they were all seated in the hut. Amar gratefully accepted a dish of roasted fish and mushrooms from Mani. It was so good to be with her again and see her safe and well. When he'd left her to return to Rajahansa, he'd been sure his death was imminent, and he would never see her again.

"So you're leaving again," Denali said to his father. "You have to take me with you. I'm not a child anymore. Frost and I defeated the whole pack of snow wolves, remember? We saved your life. We can help fight. And Aadi should come too. I don't think he should stay here with the other villagers. He's . . ."

Amar's fish turned sour on his tongue. "Does he have a fever?"

"I don't know," Denali said. "He's hiding in the jungle and won't come back to the village. I went to check on him last night, but he would not talk to me. I don't know what's wrong. He and I have been friends since I came to the palace, but it's like he's changed somehow."

Amar set his plate aside and rose to his feet. "Prepare to leave. I think we should be gone from this place before noon."

Mani scowled, and Eska gripped Kumar Raza's arm as if unwilling to let him go.

"I don't think we can go anywhere," Kumar Raza said. "Rajan's serpent can't swim across land. Kumar Raza has no dragon to fly him. And Bensharie, for all his heart, can only carry two people at a time, one on his neck and one in his back claws."

I can carry three children at a time, Bensharie interjected.

"Kumar, you are the Great Dragon Hunter," Amar said. "Work it out. We will go, and we will take Aadi, Denali, and Frost with us. They are the only possible reasons Khalid could have for coming here."

Rajan let out a dark laugh. "You're discounting the fact that he could take your wives as hostages. Could you fight him then, if you knew he would kill them if you did?"

"All right. We all go," Amar said. "Whatever it takes to keep the rest of the villagers safe."

"How?" Kumar Raza mumbled to himself. Amar could sense his mind spinning, searching for answers.

"I don't care how. I need to go help Aadi. Denali, come, show me where he is." Amar ducked out of the hut, rolled his shoulders, and stretched. Frost came out and wrapped her tail around his legs.

"This way," Denali said, motioning through the village to the other side and into the jungle beyond.

Amar rubbed Frost's dragonstone. "Let me go, little one."

It's very hot here, Frost complained.

"I know. Why aren't you with the blue dragons?"

They have a new nesting ground. Hidden. I was with Dharanidhar, but he and Kanvar made Devaj bring me here. He said I couldn't help fight the gold dragons. I've been waiting for him to come get me, but he hasn't. Frost unwound herself from Amar's legs, but flapped along beside him as he hurried into the jungle.

Amar frowned. Kanvar had said that Dharanidhar was stranded on the mountainside, blind, unable to fly, hunt or eat. Amar had promised to come help him as soon as possible, but Amar wasn't sure how he would make good on that promise.

Denali led Amar to the bank of the river that ran out into the bay. "He's usually down the riverbank that way a bit. Can you feel him?"

Amar sent his mind out in search of Aadi, but came back blank. "If he's there, he's shielding himself from me."

"He's made himself a little shelter. Just follow the riverbank and you'll find it. Should I go with you? He yelled at me last night, told me not to come bother him again."

"It's all right. You stay here, Denali. I'll go alone and see what I can do for him. Frost, you stay with Denali too."

"What's wrong with him?" Denali asked as Amar moved away.

"Rajahansa hurt him badly, and some kinds of wounds do not heal with the lick of a dragon's tongue." Amar left Denali behind and pushed his way through the thick plant growth along the river.

Less than a mile away, he came to a spot where the river bent, and a spit of land stuck out that was clear of vegetation except the large threes that grew upon it. Between two of the trees there was a wooden lean-to and a hammock hung up inside it. Aadi lay there with his arm over his face, ignoring the flies and mosquitoes buzzing around him. Faint red scars marred his chest and arms from the lesions Haidar's potion had given him. Amar winced, and his heart went out to Aadi.

"Aadi," he called softly as he approached the lean-to.

Aadi dropped his arm from his face and sat up. He frowned when he saw Amar.

"May I come in?" Amar asked.

"It's not like there's a door blocking the entrance," Aadi said.

Amar stepped into the lean-to and sat down on a stump Aadi had been using as a chair. "I did not get to speak with you when Rajahansa brought you to the mountain above Vasanti's lair. I wish I could have."

Aadi scowled. "You shouldn't have done it. You are the king. Your life is worth more than my own." His voice and eyes were hard, his fists clenched, his neck muscles tight as if he were filled to overflowing with anger, but he kept his mind firmly locked away from Amar's.

"Aadi, I have a lived a long life. You are young. You deserve to live to be my age or older. I would sacrifice my life for yours ten times over if necessary."

Aadi blinked rapidly. "But . . ."

"But?" Amar calmed his own breathing and let a sense of peace and reassurance flow from him.

Aadi jumped down from the hammock, turned his back, and crossed his arms over his chest. "But I'm not even a Naga." Bitterness laced his words.

"What makes you think that?" Amar longed to approach him, but remained seated. Aadi needed space right now and a gentle hand.

"I did not get the dragon fever. Haidar's ointment didn't work. He insisted it would work, but it didn't. I am not a Naga. I will never get the dragon fever. I will never bond to a dragon. All these years Parmver made me think I would be. All these years I've studied and worked so hard. I did everything he said. I've served you in all ways you required. But I am nothing, now. I see that. Nothing but a common human, with no power and no hope of ever being more." Aadi's voice broke. He bolted from the shelter and dove into the river.

Amar sighed and stood. By the time he got to the water, Aadi had reached the far shore. He clawed his way up the bank and vanished into the underbrush.

Aadi, Amar called to him. Aadi's shields were still up, but Amar knew where he was now. He caught hold of Aadi's mind, lowering the shields gently and forcing him to stop running.

Let me go, Aadi said. *Parmver is dead. I have no reason to stay.*

Parmver had raised Aadi from the time he was very young. They'd been like father and son. *I'm sorry. I miss him too. But he believed in you, Aadi. He was sure you are a Naga, and I am too. The fact that you did not come down with the fever doesn't mean anything beyond we were lucky enough to get the ointment washed off you in time. Every person matures at a different rate. You just need more time. That's all.*

But what if I'm right and I'm not a Naga? What if I'm like Kumar Raza and never get the fever at all? Aadi struggled to free his mind from Amar's hold. Did Aadi not realize how strong his mind already was, how well trained? Didn't he realize he could not be having this conversation with Amar if he did not have Naga blood in him? Even if he never bonded, his abilities were far beyond a normal human's. But that was not the answer Aadi needed to hear at the moment.

I will love you the same whether you ever bond or not, Amar said. *And not being a Naga does not mean you are powerless. Look what Kumar Raza has done with his life. I see in you just as much greatness as he has.*

Aadi stopped fighting. *I don't want to spend my whole life alone. Your Majesty, I am so empty, sometimes I can hardly breathe.*

Amar smiled. The symptoms were so obvious, to him at least. If Aadi did not have a fever yet, he soon would. *Come back,* he told Aadi, but put no power into it. The call was an invitation, not a command.

You still care about me? You'll still let me stay with you and serve you. Even . . . even after Rajahansa meant for me to take your place.

Rajahansa was wrong to try to force that on you, Aadi. None of that was your fault. Amar kept his anger at Rajahansa in check and shielded from Aadi's mind. *Please come back. I need you. How can I fight Khalid without your help?*

I don't think I can help. I couldn't even convince Tana she should not bond with a Great Green dragon. I tried, but she would not listen to me. Aadi felt bad about arguing with Tana. Everything that Parmver had ever taught him seemed turned on its head.

Tana is free to bond with whatever dragon she wants. The world today is not what it was when Parmver was young. Things have changed. We know more now. We understand better what it is to be a Naga. I'm sure Tana will forgive you for arguing with her. Now come back, Amar coaxed. *I don't want to have to swim across the river to come get you.*

I yelled at Denali.

Amar chuckled. *He forgives you too.*

The underbrush on the far side of the river parted and Aadi slipped into the water. He was a strong swimmer and made it halfway back to Amar's side with easy strokes, but stopped suddenly in the middle. He gasped and swam in place where he was. His eyes went vacant, and his mind slipped away from Amar's.

"Aadi," Amar yelled. He tried to get back hold of Aadi's mind but it kept slithering away from his like a serpent in water, moving fast. Amar dove into the water, swam out to Aadi and grabbed him, pulling him up under his arm while he turned on his side and swam back to shore. Aadi's mind remained blank as Amar pulled him onto the sand beside his lean-to.

Chapter Eight

Amar brushed Aadi's hair aside and pressed his hand against Aadi's damp forehead. At first Aadi's mind seemed blank, then Amar felt the sensation of swimming, sliding through the dark water, keeping to the shadows, cursing the sunlight. He was long and sleek and quick. From the shade of the trees, he lifted his head above the water and watched as the Naga Guardsmen forced the human soldiers back on their boats and set the sails. A few captured Great Blue dragons and the Great Gold dragon pride from the palace accompanied the boats.

From his hiding place in the water, he hissed and bared his fangs. *I must tell the king what is happening*, he thought.

Indumauli, Amar said in surprise.

Startled, Indumauli dove beneath the surface. *You're Majesty. I didn't feel your mind enter mine. How is it? You do not feel like yourself.*

Amar looked down at Aadi, sharing the image of the boy on the ground, gray skin, sleek black hair, eyes closed. His mind had slipped away mid-swim to join Indumauli's. *It's Aadi's mind,* Amar said. *What connection do you have with him?*

The village boy? Indumauli's mind flashed to a memory of swimming below the village, guarding it as was his duty, and seeing a toddler slip off the bank into the water. Too young to swim, the toddler was pulled under by the current and trapped against the side of the bank beneath a tree root that overhung the river. Indumauli saved the boy and lifted him up onto the bank to his mother. When the boy was a bit older, he came to the river often to swim and play with the Great Black serpent until one day he vanished from the village, taken to the palace to be with the Nagas.

Oh, Amar said. *I didn't realize you two were friends. Does his mind often slip off to visit yours?*

Not until the last couple of days, but he feels so familiar to me. I had not realized his thoughts were with me until you joined us. I hope I have not broken some law in interfering with the boy's mind.

No, Indumauli, you have not. He is close to bonding and his mind is searching for a dragon companion. It is natural, though I would have guessed his mind would go out to his gold dragon friends from the palace.

The dragons from the palace have either joined the Naga Guardsmen willingly or their minds have been taken by the Nagas. Perhaps my mind was the closest he could get to his friends.

Perhaps. Amar gritted his teeth. *But don't worry about Aadi. He's with me and I'm taking care of him.*

Amar pulled his mind back from Indumauli's and drew Aadi's back with him.

Aadi blinked, then gasped and rolled away from Amar. "Majesty, I-I was swimming."

Amar gave him a reassuring smile. "Yes, you were. You must be fond of swimming. You seem good at it."

Aadi shook his head and stood up, squeezing water from his dripping clothes. "I have not swum for years, not since Parmver brought me to the palace. Are you angry with me? I should not have run away from you. I just . . . you, and Rajahansa, and me. I feel so like . . . I did a bad thing back at the palace. The way I felt when Rajahansa touched me, it was like sunshine and power, and I wanted it. At first I didn't, I was frightened, but then he wrapped around me and I wanted to feel it, I wanted all that power. I wanted to be Rajahansa's Naga, and I knew it was wrong, but I longed for it anyway. Then it was gone. Taken away, and I was so angry. With you. With him. Angry at the whole world. And frightened. I feel so empty now. I am alone and empty, and I just want to die." Aadi's voice cracked and his body tensed, ready to run again.

Silently, Amar cursed Rajahansa, then Khalid, then Rajahansa again. "Aadi, I promise you, you will not always feel alone like you do now. And someday you will have the bond and all the power you crave. And when that time comes, you will choose what dragon you will bond with. No one else will decide for you."

"But the gold dragons are gone, taken by Khalid. I saw them on the beach." Aadi wrapped his arms around himself and shuddered.

Amar put a reassuring hand on his shoulder. "Perhaps it is not a gold dragon you are meant to bond with."

"What are you saying?" Aadi pulled out of his grasp. "Of course I will bond with a gold dragon. They are my friends, and Khalid has taken them. If I am going to be a Naga, that is, and not just a useless human, I must go to Stonefountain."

Amar smiled and glanced again at the inky black water. "Stonefountain is a long way from here, and you do not yet have a fever. Come back to the village with me. Kumar Raza and I are making plans to defeat Khalid and free the gold dragons." Amar motioned for Aadi to follow him out of the jungle. He did not feel as confident about defeating Khalid as he wanted Aadi to think he was, but that didn't matter. They had to try.

Denali and Frost waited beside the circle of huts. Denali took a tentative step forward and waited as Aadi approached just as tentatively. Denali was younger than Aadi by a couple of years but the two boys had gotten along well back at the palace. Now they eyed each other without speaking as if neither boy wanted to restart the last argument they'd had.

Frost burbled with delight, flapped over, and licked Aadi's face. That seemed to break the ice between them.

"Guess what," Denali said with a bright smile and twinkle in his eyes. "Kumar Raza's brother is going to get married. We're going to have a big celebration and a feast and everything. They've just been waiting for the king to come back and do the ceremony."

"What?" Amar said. "We don't have time for a wedding. I told them we were leaving." Of course, the woman and child on the boat. They had been...well, Amar had seen how the couple interacted with each other. He should have recognized it for what it was, but the enormity of Khalid's return had weighed too heavily on his mind. Yes, they needed to move quickly, but should he begrudge them a moment of happiness? "I wonder how long we have before Khalid's men attack this place," he muttered to himself as the boys rushed off together into the milling crowd in the center of the circle of huts.

Amar went in search of Kumar Raza and found him sharpening his sword and cleaning his armor next to Jabari's hut. Kumar Raza glanced up when Amar approached then turned his attention back to his work.

"A wedding?" Amar said. "We have to get out of here."

"Can't. Not yet. Not until Kanvar returns and can convince the Great Blue dragons to fly us to the east coast." Kumar Raza scraped the remains of what looked like cooled magma from the back of his armor. "Been trying to clean this off forever," he muttered. "Every time I think I'm done, I find more of it."

"We can't stay here that long. I can't risk these people's lives." Amar's hand went to his waist where his own sword should be hanging, but it was gone, along with his armor, jungle knives, crossbow and other gear.

"Here." Kumar Raza handed Amar his hunting knife. "It's not much. Too bad Kanvar has your sword and you gave everything else to Tana."

Amar slid the hunting knife into his belt. "She bonded with a Great Green dragon. Believe me, she needed some dragonhide armor."

Kumar Raza barked out a laugh. "A Great Green. Brave woman."

Amar scowled and rubbed his bare chest. At least his dip in the river had washed the last of the blood off him, but the stain would never come out of his pants. He squashed a wistful thought of his extensive wardrobe back at the palace. "Where's Rajan?" Amar wished he knew more about what kind of man Kumar Raza's brother was. Rajan felt powerful, yes, with an air of death and danger about him, mixed with a lilting silver softness, two opposites come together in on one man.

"The women dragged him off to get him *ready*. Dove too. The villagers have almost nothing here, but the thought of a wedding has given them something to be happy about, something to get their minds off the home they've lost." Kumar polished the last bit of armor, slid into it, and buckled it in place. "For the sake of the villagers, I think you should go through with it."

"And Rajan, you think he'll make a good father, a good husband? He feels, I don't know how to describe it, like a dormant volcano, perhaps."

"Very like that, yes."

"You're not worried."

Kumar Raza sheathed his sword and clapped Amar on the shoulder. "You're going to like Rajan. Here." He handed Amar a shirt donated by one of the villagers. The fabric was coarser than Amar was used to wearing, but he accepted it gladly and put it on.

"I suppose you've never conducted a wedding before, but you'll do fine," Kumar Raza said.

"*I* have to do it?" Amar protested as Kumar Raza led him to the front of the gathered villagers. Kumar Raza had officiated at Amar's wedding to Raza's daughter, Mani. Amar's weddings to his previous wives, who had long since passed on, had all been performed by Parmver. "I don't know how. You're the Great Dragon Hunter. You do it."

"You're the king."

"Jabari is the village leader. Let him do it."

"Amar, you've been married how many times? Surely you remember something of the ceremony." Kumar Raza planted him in front of the crowd and then stepped away.

I cannot believe we're having a wedding instead of planning a war, Amar thought. But a wedding was so much more pleasant to think about, and the idea that normal life would go on even with Khalid back in the world gave him a bit of comfort. Kumar Raza was right; it would probably comfort the villagers as well.

Mani smiled at him from the front of the crowd, her mind going back to the day the two of them had wed. It was a good day, the happiest in Amar's life. They'd joined hands and hearts in front of Kumar Raza and many of the other dragon hunters in front of the grand mansion at the Varnan colony in Kundiland. The spray of the fountain in the yard had filled the air with music. Purple orchids, flame hearts, and shooting stars were draped in garlands from the walls. The evening was lit with tin lanterns cut so the light played across the ground in the shape of gold dragons. Amar had liked that touch, though it meant more to him and Rajahansa than the humans present.

The thought of Rajahansa twisted Amar's heart back to the present. Rajahansa was gone, lost to him, his mind and soul first, and then his body. Best not to think of it. Best not to remember his life before.

Bensharie purred in the back of his mind. *You are not alone, and you will yet have a good life again.*

Amar acknowledged Bensharie's encouragement as Rajan, dressed in the mottled green clothes of the villagers, stepped out from one of the huts. His hair was cut and tamed into submission. His beard shaved. He looked less dangerous and more human. Dove came out of another hut. The women had done even more with her. She wore a purple dress that had been dyed to look like it was fashioned from flower petals. Her hair was pulled up on top of her head and accented with flowers and glittering flakes of mica. She looked as beautiful as any bride had ever been. Little Eleanor walked beside her, dressed to match her mother. As Dove approached Rajan and their eyes met, pink tinged her cheeks. They were in love; Amar could feel that beyond any doubt. He smiled at them as they held out their hands to clasp in front of him.

He put his hand overtop theirs. Rajan's mind was veiled from him, but Dove's surged with devotion, love, and admiration for Rajan. Amar caught glimpses of Rajan, bruised and battered from a giant wave, working tirelessly to free survivors from mud and wreckage. Rajan far off atop a wall, calling a swarm of blood-lusted raptors to him to keep them from attacking Dove and his friends. Rajan was fearless in the face of danger and yet gentle enough to gather Eleanor in his arms and hold her as if she were his own child. Perhaps Amar had judged Rajan wrong, but all Amar had known of him was a Naga powerful enough to take over the Maran senate, a Naga who had stirred the humans into a frenzy to come to Kundiland and destroy Amar's family and home.

All the hurt and pain caused by Rajan's actions crashed in on Amar and no words would pass his lips. Kumar Raza had taken it for granted that Amar would forgive his brother and accept him as part of the family. In better days that would have been so easy. Amar's mind flashed with memories of the pain as the dragon hunters tore the life from Rajahansa. The wounds so fresh, it had only been a day since he'd suffered them, but he doubted he'd be able to forget in a lifetime. He pulled his hand away and turned his back on the couple, struggling to get control of himself. This wasn't Rajan's fault. None of this had been Rajan's fault. The red dragon had sent him to Maran, and it was Khalid who had turned Rajahansa to evil, not Kumar Raza's brother.

Behind him, the crowd started to shift and murmur.

He balled his hands into fists. The pain wouldn't leave him. He'd never had trouble forgiving any hurt or wrong done him before. Why now? Had the darkness in Raja-hansa's mind affected him as well? Anger and pain and darkness. He closed his eyes as the crowd grew more restless. He felt Kumar Raza break away and come toward him, but Bensharie reached him first.

Amar. Bensharie landed beside him.

Amar reached for Bensharie as if Bensharie could banish all the darkness and pain. *I can't do this. I need time to think.* Bensharie bent down so Amar could climb on his back and then launched into the air, circling above the village.

Frowning, Kumar Raza stared up at them for a moment. Amar shielded his mind from his old friend. He did not want to know what Kumar thought at that moment. A salty breeze blew up off the ocean, stinging his cheeks.

Below him, Kumar Raza placed his hand atop Rajan and Dove's and led them through their vows, doing what Amar had been unable to.

"I failed them. I couldn't do it," Amar whispered. "They needed a king, and I . . . I am nothing."

You are hurt. They can see that. No man could recover so quickly. Give yourself time to heal, Bensharie said. *Listen to your own words. What you said about Aadi is true. Some wounds can't be healed with a lick of the tongue.*

Amar bowed his head. The knot in his throat drove him to silence. The ceremony played out below and the festivities began. Beaming, Rajan and Dove retreated to one of the huts, leaving Eleanor in Eska and Mani's care. Denali, Frost, and Miki scampered about nearly toppling the table of fruit that had been set out and got scolded by Jabari. Aadi kept to himself in the shadows at the edge of the huts.

Bensharie settled on the beach away from the village and folded his wings. Amar dismounted and slumped to the sand beside him.

Your Majesty, Tana's soft voice came to Amar's mind. *Your Majesty can you hear me? Vasanti said you left before dawn. I'm sorry, I've slept all morning. Where are you? Do you need help?*

I'm at the new village, Amar responded, glad to have something to take his mind off his failure in the village. *But we'll be moving soon. When I figure out where we're going, I'll tell you so you and Vasanti can meet us there. How are her little ones?*

They're fine. She hunted for them this morning. Right now they're playing hide and seek in the lair. Tana found Vasanti's wyrmlings delightful and wished she could have been there to watch them hatch.

Amar came close to a smile. The hatching had been a happy occasion.

A cry of surprise went up from the villagers, and Amar snapped his gaze toward the huts. The flap of great wings pounded the air. An enormous, battered, Great Blue dragon swooped down into the center of the village, dropped something from his hind claw, and settled to the ground.

Chapter Nine

Kumar Raza had never been gladder to see Dharanidhar in his life. The giant blue dragon was the answer to most of the issues Kumar had been trying to solve. He wasn't so glad to see General Chandran, on the other hand. Dharanidhar must have thought Chandran was an ally, but Kumar Raza wasn't so sure.

General Chandran got to his feet and brushed the dirt from his blue dragonhide armor. After straightening the gold braid at his shoulder, his hand went to his sword hilt. He moved away from Dharanidhar while looking about at the villagers as if trying to decide why none of them were running in fear from the Great Blue dragon. Miki raced over to Dharanidhar, jumped up on his leg, and licked his scales. The look on Chandran's face said, "Since when did dogs get along with dragons?"

Still cheerful from the wedding, the humans moved their celebration into the edge of the jungle away from the dragon.

Sensing General Chandran's consternation, Kumar Raza chuckled and stepped through the departing crowd. "General Chandran, what a pleasant surprise." His own hand settled on his sword hilt as well, just in case Chandran was not prepared to ally himself with the Naga King.

General Chandran's eyes widened as Kumar Raza strode up to him, followed by Frost who chirped loudly and flapped forward to land in between them.

"Don't blind him, Frost," Kumar said, realizing the young dragon had decided Chandran was an enemy.

Frost hissed and spread her wings.

Kumar shot his hand down to cover her forehead at the moment that Frost's dragonstone flashed despite Kumar Raza's order.

"Ouch. What in the world?" General Chandran blinked and rubbed his eyes.

"She's a Great White dragon," Kumar Raza said. "You're lucky I blocked most of that. She's still young enough it wouldn't have blinded you permanently, but your vision would most certainly have been damaged. I'd suggest you take your hand off your sword before she freezes you to a block of ice."

General Chandran lifted his hand away from his sword and shot Kumar Raza a look of utter bewilderment. "A Great White in Kundiland?"

"Denali," Kumar Raza called to his son. "Why don't you take Frost down to the beach and play for a while."

"Sure. Come on Frost." Denali motioned to his dragon and headed for the beach.

Frost hissed at General Chandran one more time then flapped off after him.

"And Miki too." Kumar Raza decided it would be best not to point out to General Chandran that the dog had saddled up beside him and lifted his leg to urinate on his boots.

Denali called for Miki and the dog bounded away.

"I'm sorry, General," Kumar Raza said. "That was my son Denali and his . . . friends."

"A Great White dragon?" General Chandran dropped his hand back down to his sword. Dharanidhar let out a warning growl. "Maybe you should just take the sword," Chandran told Kumar Raza, "before I get eaten alive."

Kumar Raza waved away the thought. "No need. I feel safe. If you were crazy enough to think you could best me in a sword fight, it would only add more entertainment to my day."

General Chandran glared at him. "I don't find today entertaining at all. Do you realize what's happened?"

Kumar Raza let the smile fade from his face. "I know what's happened. Khalid has returned and is in command of an army of Nagas from the far side of the world. I intend to move quickly to combat this threat. It seems

Dharanidhar thought you might like to join the fight as my ally. Is that so?"

General Chandran glanced around him, taking in all the details of the village like any good soldier before speaking. "How is it you communicate so well with these Great dragons? Where's Kanvar? I know he's bound to the blue one."

"I have sent Kanvar to procure us some singing stones that Khalid can't control."

"How is it Khalid could do anything with the others? The stones are supposed to block Naga powers."

"You've been to Darvat, General. I know you've seen what only Raahi and Karishi have seen. The singing stones were the tormented spirits of the dead from Stonefountain, and Khalid's spirit has resided in the fountain for a thousand years. A spirit link goes far beyond normal Naga powers."

"You sent Kanvar to Darvat?"

"Yes."

"And Khalid is not linked to those gems."

"Correct."

"Does he know about them?"

"Unfortunately, yes. We can only hope Kanvar reaches Darvat before the other Nagas," Kumar Raza said.

"How can he if his dragon is here?" General Chandran pointed over his shoulder at Dharanidhar.

Kumar's gaze flicked to Dharanidhar who had sunk to the ground. His joints looked swollen and sore. The thought struck Kumar that Dharanidhar was blind, how in the world had he flown to the village? He stared up at Dharanidhar's milky orbs and realized with a jolt that a lesser green serpent was curled around Dharanidhar's neck with its head and stubby forelegs resting between Dharanidhar's eyes.

"Dharanidhar?" Kumar Raza said with surprise, pointing up at the serpent. Was the blue dragon seeing through the serpent's eyes?

Dharanidhar grinned and nodded. Blue fire crackled between his jaws.

"You are ignoring my questions," General Chandran snapped.

"My apologies." Kumar turned his attention back to the general. "Frost is here because I spent twelve years in the Great North searching for the Great White dragons. In the process, I fell in love, got married, and had a son. Frost's parents died of starvation and we've adopted her into our family. Kanvar is flying with a gold dragon to Darvat because . . . Dharanidhar is needed here." No sense revealing the true state of the Great Blue dragon's health.

"And your plans once you get the stones?" General Chandran was all business. Fine, he had a right to be. Kumar could deal with that.

"My strategy has not been finalized yet. I've been waiting for Dharanidhar to arrive, since he's been on the east coast and knows what's been happening there. Our first order of business is, of course, to get out of this village. It's indefensible and Khalid knows its location. But where to go and where to strike first, that's something I'll decide after I get Dharanidhar's report."

Kumar Raza gazed across the beach to where Bensharie had landed on the sand. In the direct sunlight, he could not see Bensharie or Amar who had to be under his wing or on the other side of him. But Kumar could feel them both. Amar was out there, still agitated as he had been before the wedding, and General Chandran had led the dragon hunters to kill Rajahansa. Kumar could not be sure how Chandran would react to finding out Amar was alive, or how Amar would react to the man who had just yesterday tried to kill him.

Kumar flicked his eyes to the hut where Rajan and Dove had gone. The odds were good Rajan would not come out for a while. Good thing, Chandran might respond violently to the Naga that had taken over his country. Chandran's arrival had created a delicate situation and Kumar wasn't sure which way to step.

When Kumar turned his attention back to General Chandran, the general had folded his arms across his chest. The look in his eyes said he'd followed Kumar Raza's gaze and figured there was more going on here than Kumar had said. "Then shouldn't you get paper and ink for the dragon?"

"Paper and ink?" Kumar Raza's mind spun. There was unlikely to be any in the village.

"Yes, so you can get the dragon's report of what he's seen." General Chandran scoffed. "He's blind. What do you think he saw?"

"He saw well enough to snatch you away from the Nagas or you'd be enslaved with the rest of your army."

General Chandran shook his head. "Raza, be straight with me. I'm not stupid. If Kanvar isn't here, then some other Naga must be here or you wouldn't be able to communicate with the dragons. It can't be Denali if he's your son not your grandson. Besides, he's too young. Is it Tana? Dharanidhar hinted there were Nagas I don't know about. Who are they and how strong? Can we count on them to stay on our side and not double cross us to Khalid?"

"I'm a Naga." Aadi's voice cut across the air. He moved away from the shadows of the hut where he'd been standing close enough to listen to Kumar Raza's conversation and strode over to the two men.

Kumar gritted his teeth. He did not know Aadi well, but the boy had obviously sensed Kumar Raza's wish to keep knowledge of the king and Rajan secret for now.

"You?" General Chandran looked Aadi up and down.

Aadi raised his chin defiantly. "You don't believe me?"

General Chandran frowned. "You're rather young."

"I'm old enough. Dharanidhar, what did you see?"

Dharanidhar's dragonstone flashed. A look of intense concentration came over Aadi's face. He stood with eyes locked on Dharanidhar for a long moment before speaking.

"The Nagas are forcing your soldiers back onto the boats. There are four Great Blue dragons under Naga control and what's left of the gold dragon pride."

That's not enough information, Kumar Raza realized. It was nothing more than he already knew. He thanked Aadi anyway. The boy would be a powerful Naga once he bonded, his impressions from Dharanidhar's mind were far more exact than Kumar had gotten.

General Chandran glanced out toward where Bensharie hid on the beach. "You intend for Kanvar's dragon to fly us out of here, I suppose?"

"I would like several more of the Great Blue dragons to join us. Dharanidhar, will the pride join our fight against Khalid?"

Dharanidhar shook his head. His dragonstone flashed. Kumar Raza understood the impression behind his words but left the interpretation for Aadi to share.

"No," Aadi said. "They will not go anywhere near the Nagas without the singing stones. Their nesting ground is hidden and they wish it to remain that way."

"Thank you, Aadi," Kumar Raza said. He wondered how General Chandran would react to the knowledge that Kumar had Naga blood in him and could communicate with the dragons on a rudimentary level of his own. But there was no need to give out that information with Aadi playing the part so well.

From the beach, Bensharie let out a startled roar and flapped in agitation, creating a visible ripple above the ground.

"Is that your dragon?" General Chandran asked Aadi. His hand closed on his sword hilt and half-drew it out. "What's wrong? What's he saying?"

Aadi's eyes widened. "Amar says Indumauli's in the river beside the Maran Colony. Five of the Naga Guardsmen, one ship, and a garrison of soldiers stayed behind when the fleet sailed. He overheard the Nagas talking. They are planning to attack this village tomorrow and kill everyone."

"*Amar* said that?" General Chandran's voice was acidic.

Kumar Raza gritted his teeth. In his surprise at the news, Aadi had slipped. There would be no covering the truth now.

"Yes. He says we have to leave the village now. Kumar, you have to think of a way to get the Nagas to come after us instead of the villagers." Aadi blundered on, not realizing yet what he'd done.

General Chandran drew his sword and headed out of the village toward the beach and Bensharie.

Kumar Raza grabbed Aadi's arm to keep him from saying anything else. "Go get Rajan," he ordered. Then he drew his own sword and went after General Chandran. He caught him halfway between the village and Bensharie, grabbed his arm, swung him around, and leveled his sword at him.

Chandran knocked Kumar's sword aside with his own.

Kumar Raza pulled back, circling to put himself in between General Chandran and Amar. "You don't want to fight me, General."

"I don't think you're as good as everyone makes you out to be. It's all stories blown out of proportion. You're just a man. And not a young man anymore." General Chandran set his own stance. He was a soldier, a fighter, and not frightened of Kumar Raza.

"You're not young either," Kumar said. "But I wasn't referring to my chance of defeating you. What I mean is, we need each other to help fight Khalid."

General Chandran's face twisted into a grimace. "I have no way of knowing if that's truly your intent, and neither do you. With the Nagas here, neither of us can know or trust our own mind. We're their playthings, Kumar, like a mouse caught in a kitrat's paws. Sure, they'll let us run around thinking we're free for a moment, but then they'll pounce, and it will be all over. Well, if I've only got a moment, I'm going to bite as hard as I can."

Chandran thrust his sword at Kumar. Kumar blocked and Chandran thrust again.

Kumar Raza parried his attack. "I won't let you hurt Amar." Any more than he and the dragon hunters had already.

"Because he has control of your mind."

"No." Kumar was surprised at how good of a swordsman Chandran was. That would make this easier. "Because

I know him, and I trust him. All he's ever wanted is to live in peace with the humans, and all he wants now is to see Khalid stopped."

"You're a fool." Steel clashed as the two swords met and parted. "The blue dragon said that Khalid had taken Devaj, and Devaj is Amar's son. He will not kill his own son. He will not put the freedom of the humans over the life of his son."

"You think so? Even though you know he ordered Kanvar and Tana to end his own life in an attempt to stop Khalid."

"Any father would die for his children. No man will kill his own son. Believe me, I had sons, and do you know who killed them? That monster behind us. The blue dragons tore them down and burned their bodies to ash." General Chandran's blows became more ferocious.

Kumar Raza's muscles burned. He was stiff and out of shape from his long time in the small boat, but he fought back hard. "Perhaps Kanvar's trust in you was misplaced." Kumar twisted aside Chandran's blade and lunged forward, his sword hit Chandran's chest and would have drawn blood if Chandran had not been wearing armor.

Chandran twisted away before the sword could pierce the dragon scales. The tip scraped to the side, leaving a white scratch across his armor. His sword came up un-hindered, and Kumar Raza had to jump back to keep from being sliced across the neck. Out of the corner of his eye,

Kumar saw Rajan skid to a stop in the sand out of General Chandran's sight. He looked questioningly at Kumar as if asking whether he should interfere or let his brother go on enjoying the battle.

Kumar shook his head. General Chandran feared the Nagas controlling him. If they were ever to gain him as an ally, they needed to leave his mind alone. And Chandran needed proof that they would. Kumar planned to give him that proof. *Stay out of this Rajan*, Kumar thought to his brother. *I need you to protect the king, with your sword if necessary, but not your mind. Do not interfere. I know what I'm doing.*

Rajan raised an eyebrow then sauntered off toward Amar and Bensharie.

Kumar Raza redoubled his efforts against General Chandran, parrying and attacking, driving the general back.

"Get him, Dad." Denali ran up with Frost and Miki. "Stick him like a walrus. We'll roast him for dinner." Miki barked in agreement.

Frowning, Aadi came up beside Denali.

A half smile crossed General Chandran's face. "Children," he muttered. And Kumar Raza sensed in him a feeling of fatherly love and devotion. A picture of Kanvar flitted through Chadran's mind so strongly even Kumar with his limited abilities could see a fuzzy image of Kanvar cleaning Chandran's armor, of Kanvar attempting to load the cumbersome crossbow he'd saved for years to purchase. Perhaps Kanvar was wrong about General Chandran ever being able to live side-by-side with the Nagas, but Kumar Raza had no doubt that General Chandran loved Kanvar as if he were his own son.

Kumar Raza faltered and let the grip of his sword hand slacken so that when he blocked Chandran's next blow, his sword flew out of his hands, spinning and glimmering in the sunlight before it thumped into the sand at Denali's feet.

Denali cried out in surprise and snatched up his father's sword, but it was too late, General Chandran already had his sword pressed to Kumar Raza's throat.

"Go ahead," Kumar Raza said. "Do it. Kill me."

General Chandran glared and twisted his wrist so the blade cut into Kumar's flesh, drawing blood. Amar and Rajan walked up to stand beside Denali and Aadi. No one made any move to stop Chandran from ending Kumar Raza's life.

Seeing Rajan, General Chandran's hand jerked in surprise, cutting Kumar deeper. "Stay where you are," Chandran ordered, instinctively pulling Kumar around in front of him with the sword still to his throat as a hostage. "I'll kill him if you do anything. Don't think I won't."

Rajan folded his arms across his chest. Amar clenched his fists. Denali bit his lip and said nothing, but kept one hand on Frost and one on Miki. Aadi shuddered and walked away.

"You're a soldier," Kumar Raza said. "I know you won't hesitate to kill. So what are you waiting for? Finish it."

"You want me to kill you?" Chandran's mind flashed again to Kanvar, wondering if Kanvar would ever forgive him for killing his grandfather.

Kumar Raza took a deep breath, trying to ignore the burn in his throat, the blood trickling down his chest, and his own fear of dying. "I want you to know that you can. No one is stopping you. You have no singing stone and yet the Nagas, despite their love for me, are not stopping you. Your mind is free to do as you like."

"Perhaps they *want* you dead." The blade shook in Chandran's hand, adding depth to the cut already in Kumar's throat.

"Amar is my son-in-law and best friend. Rajan is my twin brother. I assure you, they don't want me dead. They do want you as an ally, of your own free will, on your terms. They will give you their oath not to interfere with your mind if you will agree to help us fight Khalid." Kumar Raza held his breath. By the fountain, he hoped Kanvar was right about General Chandran.

"And afterward?" General Chandran asked. "After Khalid is dead. What then? It is my duty to destroy Nagas. I will have no choice but to kill you all. Even you Raza, if your brother is a Naga, then you have Naga blood as well."

Rajan scowled. Amar's eyes held a cold look that Kumar had never before seen on his face. Kumar knew his friend was hurting but was at a loss at what to do about it. It would have to be dealt with sooner or later, but not now.

"I like your optimism, General," Kumar Raza said. "I'm glad to know you are certain we will defeat Khalid and have an after to worry about. But why don't we leave after for after? I'm sure Amar understands that once Khalid falls you'll go back to trying to kill him, and he'll go back to attempting to stay alive."

"How?" General Chandran's voice turned sharper than his sword as he spoke to Amar and Rajan. "How did you stay alive? Both your dragons are dead. I saw their bodies, and I know how the bond works between Nagas and dragons. You can't be standing here, either of you."

Amar and Rajan said nothing, obeying Kumar Raza's orders to stay out of this.

"Answer me!" General Chandran shouted.

Kumar Raza grew light headed and wondered exactly how much blood he'd lost. From the pale look on Denali's face, much more than was good for him. "They each bonded with a new dragon the moment before their old one died," Kumar said. "Chandran, there's a child present. Kill me or let me go."

"I'll have the oaths first," Chandran said. Good, he was considering being reasonable.

Amar stepped forward and held out his right hand. "By the fountain and by my life and soul, I will not interfere with your mind or force you to do anything against your will."

"And you?" Chandran said to Rajan, pressing the sword even tighter into Kumar's neck. "You tried to take over the world. How is it you've sided with Amar instead of Khalid? I do not believe I can ever trust you."

Rajan's mind reached for Chandran's. He could make the general trust him. He should do it now before his brother bled to death. Chandran would never know Rajan was influencing him.

Don't do it, Kumar ordered him.

Rajan's fist clenched on his sword hilt. "If you kill my brother, I swear I'll do things to your mind so hideous that you will not only beg for death, you'll wish you never lived. And if you free him now I'll leave your feeble mind to its own pitiful devices. I swear by all the fires of the volcano you will be free from my control as long as you make no move to hurt any of the people I hold dear. Not counting Devaj, since we have no choice but to fight him."

"What about the other Naga? The boy?" General Chandran said. "And Tana?"

"He can't hurt you. He hasn't boded yet," Kumar said. Black specks began to appear in front of his eyes. "Tana's a long way from here. She can't touch your mind." He swallowed, but that only made the sword cut him deeper. Still, General Chandran held him prisoner. He was bleeding. He was dying. Growing dizzy, he realized Chandran was waiting to see if the Nagas would keep their oath. "Don't wait to long," he muttered.

Neither Rajan nor Amar made a move to control General Chandran.

Chandran eased the sword away from Kumar Raza's throat and let him fall to his knees. Frost rushed to him and licked his throat frantically.

"You let me win, didn't you," General Chandran said in disgust. "Just to prove your point. What kind of a man are you?"

"I'm the Great Dragon Hunter," Kumar Raza said.

Chapter Ten

Amar unclenched his fists and went to Kumar Raza's side. The smell of blood sickened him—the way it slicked Kumar Raza's red armor and dripped onto the white sand, staining the ground. Kumar must be dead-certain an alliance with General Chandran was necessary to risk his life in this fashion to get it. Amar pushed his way past Frost and Miki to Kumar Raza's side and helped him to his feet.

Denali still had his father's sword. He stepped between Kumar Raza and General Chandran and took up a fighting stance with it. Frost flapped to his side.

"Frost and I haven't taken any kind of oath," Denali said. "You touch my father again, and we'll kill you. I don't care how good of a swordsman you are. I'll kill you."

Kumar wavered in Amar's hands. He'd lost a lot of blood, but he was still conscious, and he didn't call Denali off. He had too much trust in the General for Amar's liking. Amar wished he could look into Chandran's mind to see if he intended to fight with Denali, but honoring his oath, he kept a shield up between his mind and Chandran's.

Rajan stepped up behind Denali and drew his own sword. His lips were pressed together and his eyes blazed, leaving no question as to his intent. If Chandran made any move toward the boy, he'd fight Rajan as well. Rajan's oath did not hold him from slicing Chandran down with his sword. But Amar got the disturbing impression from Rajan's mind that his mouth was watering to tear General Chandran's throat out with his bare teeth instead of using the sword.

Amar shuddered and helped Kumar Raza down to the water where he could wash the blood away. "Good luck explaining that scar to Eska," Amar said.

Kumar Raza choked out a weak laugh. "Good thing the women were on the other side of the village." He waded into the water up to his chest to wash the blood away. "Drat, now I'm going to have to clean the salt off my armor again."

Back up the beach, General Chandran wiped the blood off his sword and sheathed it. Without a word to Denali and Frost, Chandran retreated to the village, passing Aadi who had gone back to stand in the shadow of the closest hut, as if he, like a black serpent, would wither up and die in direct sunlight.

Is Raza all right? Aadi's mind questioned. He was not strong enough yet to speak directly into Amar's mind, but if Amar initiated contact, the two of them could converse like they had at the river.

He's dizzy and has a headache, but he'll survive. Amar walked beside Kumar Raza back toward the village. Kumar was a little unsteady but managed to stay on his feet.

Will he forgive me? Aadi slipped back farther into the shadows when he saw Kumar Raza and Amar headed toward him.

Forgive you for what? Amar asked.

I interrupted his conversation with General Chandran. I thought I could help; he seemed to need my help, but...I accidentally let out you were alive. Kumar Raza was trying to keep that secret. Aadi continued his retreat around to the far side of the hut as Amar approached it.

I sense no anger at you in his mind. In fact, all I feel from him is an irritating smug satisfaction.

Aadi laughed. It was a pathetically weak laugh, but Amar was glad to hear it. He wanted to believe that Aadi had started to recover. Amar's concern for the villagers resurged now that he was sure Kumar Raza would live.

General Chandran waited for them just inside the circle of huts. Amar stopped in front of him and gritted his teeth to remain silent until Rajan and Denali joined them. He wanted to send Denali away, but sensed a fierce determination in the boy.

"Aadi told you what Indumauli said?" Amar asked Kumar Raza once they'd all gathered.

"Yes." Kumar Raza's face was pale and he had a brilliant red scar across his neck.

"What should we do? I don't think our leaving here will save the villagers." Amar fought to keep his mind from panic.

Kumar raked his fingers through his beard. "We have to attack them first, by dawn tomorrow at the latest."

"They have a garrison of soldiers," Amar said. "And we don't have any singing stones yet. Even together our minds aren't strong enough to overcome five Nagas. Maybe if Kanvar were here. I don't think any of us can match him for raw power right now." *Sorry, Bensharie, but you're just not that strong yet, and that silver serpent I sense swimming around in the bay isn't either.*

Bensharie had stayed out on the beach away from the village. He still felt sick from the images of Kumar bleeding he had seen in Amar's mind. Bensharie acknowledged Amar's point that together they were not as strong as Amar and Rajahansa had been.

"Kanvar might be powerful," Rajan said to Amar. "But you and I are older and better trained for battle."

"I'm not trained for battle." Amar's chest tightened with fear at the thought of attacking five trained Naga Guardsmen and a garrison of soldiers. "All I've trained to use my powers for is to protect, comfort, and heal."

"You're a dragon hunter," Kumar Raza said.

"I don't even like killing lesser dragons. I only did it because you made me so I could marry Mani." Yes, he'd acted the part of a dragon hunter out of love for his wife, but that did not give him the training or skill to fight intelligent creatures.

Rajan shook his head. "Listen to him, Kumar. He's incapable of fighting. That just leaves you and me."

"And me," Denali interrupted.

"And the kid. Attacking the Maran garrison is insane. We must get the villagers to go into the jungle and hide."

"And Tana," Denali said.

Rajan glared at him.

"Tana's dragon is a rather fierce fighter," Kumar Raza said.

"She'll be slaughtered," Rajan countered. "And she has wyrmlings. You want them to grow up parentless like Frost here?"

"Stop," Amar ordered. He had enough turmoil in his own head; he didn't need an argument between Kumar and Rajan as well. "Kumar says attack. Rajan says hide. General Chandran, do you think we have any chance against that garrison?"

"It's my fortress and those are my men. I don't relish the idea of killing my own people." General Chandran caressed his sword hilt and paced away from the group and back. "How long until Kanvar gets here with the singing stones?"

"Three days at the soonest. Most likely four or five," Amar said. He felt trapped. Khalid had outsmarted them in every direction.

"Look," Kumar Raza said. "We just have to attack the garrison. We don't have to win or capture it. We just have to attack it and pull back. Attack it and pull back. Keep the Naga Guardsmen pinned there in defense of their own fortress so they can't fly out here to the village. All we have to do is keep them busy until Kanvar arrives."

"What about our wives and children?" Rajan said. "I'm not leaving Dove here by herself. If even one Naga slips past us, he'll come for our families and use them against us. We can't risk them being killed or taken has hostages."

Amar flushed. Rajan had only been married less than an hour. Of course he wouldn't want to fly off and leave Dove and Eleanor alone. Amar didn't want to leave Mani again either. Hide or fight? Go or stay? If only they could do both, but splitting up what small force they had would certainly cause both ventures to fail.

I think there is a way to do both. Bensharie landed behind Amar and put a reassuring foreclaw on his shoulder. *Dharanidhar, can you fly now? Is the medicine working?*

Amar realized the villagers had given Dharanidhar a dose of his medicine while Kumar Raza and Chandran had been fighting.

The Great Blue dragon had curled up to rest in the center of the village and several of the village children were tossing fish heads up to the lesser green serpent perched on his head. Dharanidhar shifted and stretched his wings. *I can fly now.* Dharanidhar glanced over at Bensharie, and Amar realized with a start that Dharanidhar was seeing through the lesser dragon's eyes. Of course, it made sense. Amar felt foolish for not having thought of that option sooner, but then he'd never considered taking control of anything's mind for his own personal uses.

Kivi doesn't mind. He likes me. Of course, that might be just because I didn't eat him. Dharanidhar grinned.

"What are the dragons saying?" Chandran demanded.

"Hold on. I'm not sure yet," Amar said.

The villagers were winding down their celebration and headed back to their huts a few at a time. There was still so much work to do to rebuild their lives.

There's a platform inside a net Elkatran was using to carry villagers and supplies, Bensharie said. *I'm sure Dharanidhar could carry far more than Elkatran could. You could all fit on the platform. Silverwave, Rajan and his family, Mani, Eska, Denali, and Miki. I can carry you and Aadi. General Chandran and Kumar Raza can ride on Dharanidhar's back.*

"Elkatran never could have carried so much," Amar said aloud, so General Chandran would have some hint as to what they were talking about.

He only took one family and their belongings at a time. But Dharanidhar is huge compared to Elkatran. I'm sure everyone will be a bit squished on the platform, but I think Dhar could do it, Bensharie insisted.

Dharanidhar rose to his feet. *To what end, Little Poet? Where could I possibly take them that they'd be safe?*

Amar's mind spun. "Vasanti's lair, perhaps."

No, Bensharie said. *Devaj knows where Vasanti's lair is, which means Khalid knows and the Naga Guardsmen know. They'll check for us there before they come to the village. But does anyone know where Karishi is?*

"In the mountain by the village last I heard," Amar said.

Exactly. Bensharie flapped into the air in excitement. *Somewhere in the mountain. Devaj does not know where. Just before we took the last villagers away, Karishi said he was going to seal himself in the mountain and never come out again. I doubt he meant never, permanently, but I know he believed that no one could reach him there.*

"We take the women and children to Karishi?" Amar said. If Amar could reach Karishi's mind, he could convince him to open the mountain for them and close it up again.

Right. We tell the villagers to hide in the jungle for a few days, just in case. Take your families to Karishi, and set up a base at the old jungle village where we can prepare to launch our attack. Vasanti can meet us there, and Karishi can take her wyrmlings into the mountain with the other children. Benshari let out an excited roar.

Kumar Raza grimaced. "I didn't follow most of that."

"Nor I," General Chandran said with a scowl. "It seems when I'm around Nagas I only ever get half a conversation."

"Bensharie has a plan I think might work," Amar said. The others listened intently as he explained Bensharie's idea.

"Brilliant," Kumar Raza said. "I knew there was some piece of information I was missing. Karishi."

"Wrong," General Chandran said. "There's more than one bit of information you don't have. Qadim and nine of his most elite dragon hunters are at the village. Kanvar's dragon dropped them off there before coming here. You may have convinced me to fight alongside you, but you won't convince them."

Amar's heart fell. He wanted to have some place to feel safe and gather his forces for battle against Khalid.

Rajan grinned, showing his disturbingly sharp teeth. "I don't see that as a problem. They haven't got any singing stones. They'll be an asset to us. We'll have more than Kumar and Chandran who can really fight. What garrison could possibly stand against the Great Dragon Hunter and ten of his lackeys?"

"Rajan," Amar snapped. Then he bit his lip and took a moment to calm himself before continuing. "You gave an oath to General Chandran."

"That I wouldn't interfere with *his* mind. Doesn't mean I can't control the rest of the bloodthirsty mob."

"No. I mean, yes it does. We need the humans to be our allies, not our puppets." Amar looked to Kumar Raza for some clue how to rein in his brother.

Kumar Raza shook his head. "Qadim will never join us willingly. I doubt we can even get to Karishi without dealing with the dragon hunters if they're in the village. We need to choose a new plan or let Rajan keep them from interfering with this one."

All eyes fell on Amar. He was the king. "I cannot condone enslaving the minds of the dragon hunters for any cause. Qadim is my friend. I've hunted with him so many times."

"Qadim is your enemy." Rajan reached into Amar's mind and pulled his memory of Qadim's brutal slaying of Rajahansa to the front of his mind. For a moment Amar relived the pain, the terror, and the desolation of those moments.

Amar gasped and stumbled backward against Bensharie. Bensharie growled a warning and shoved Rajan out of Amar's mind.

"Rajan." Amar lifted a shaking hand. "I will not break all the vows of my youth. Just because I must face evil does not mean that I will succumb to it. I am not Khalid."

Rajan's face went scarlet. "You would leave your wife above ground where she could be slaughtered just because you're too *nice* to take control of violent men who want to kill you? Such pride. Such hubris. Stay here and die then. I will not throw my family's life away." Rajan stalked off to the hut where he'd left Dove.

Rajan's right, Kumar Raza thought, but he kept his mouth shut. General Chandran's face was stone cold. Amar did not enter his mind to see what he was thinking.

"Dharanidhar," Amar said. "Prepare to fly us to the ledge above the jungle village. We can meet with Karishi there, hopefully without the dragon hunters noticing. We'll avoid the village and go directly from the cliff to attack the Maran colony."

What about Rajan? Dharanidhar asked. Bensharie had already flown off to fetch the moving platform. Frost flapped up to perch on Dharanidhar's shoulders and Denali went to look for his mother.

"I don't know," Amar said. "Kumar, will you go see if you can talk some sense into him?"

Kumar Raza squared his shoulders and walked off after Rajan.

General Chandran cleared his throat. "Kanvar tried to tell me what type of man you are. I did not believe him . . . until now. I'm glad I got to meet you." Chandran held out his hand to Amar.

Amar clasped it in his own and gave it a hardy shake. "And I you. I did not believe Kanvar when he said you were a human with a fair mind. I know he thinks of you as more of a father than he does me. I'm glad to see his trust in you is not misplaced. Someone like Qadim would not have hesitated to kill Kumar once he learned that his brother was a Naga."

General Chandran pulled his hand away and clenched it into a fist. "I am the supreme commander of the Maran army. It is my job to do whatever it takes to protect my people's freedom. If that means making an alliance with one Naga to destroy a more dangerous one, so be it. But after . . . I make no promises for after. As long as I am General, I must follow my orders from the Maran Senate. And right now those orders are to kill every Naga I find. I'm sorry, Amar. I see now you are nothing like Khalid. But I want no misunderstanding between us. This alliance is only temporary."

"So be it," Amar agreed.

Chapter Eleven

Kanvar watched the ocean waves rolling below him—
gentle swells with little white caps where the evening
breeze caught the tops of them. This crossing from Varna
to Darvat was so much easier than his last had been. Vivid
memories of the hurricane that had torn Dharanidhar from
the sky blistered Kanvar's mind: the crushing pain as
Dharanidhar's hind legs slammed against the rocks on the
Fifth Finger, the despair of being stranded thirsty and
helpless. Kanvar sucked in a hard breath. Dharanidhar had
never recovered from the hurt he'd taken last time Kanvar
had flown to Darvat.

"You're tense," Lord Theodoric said from behind
Kanvar on Ishayu's back. "Are you expecting some sort of
danger?"

"I don't know what to expect. I'm hoping for a nice
visit with a close friend and then . . ." Kanvar's father had

not told Lord Theodoric why they were going to Darvat. The Hall of Raahi's ancestors had remained secret until Karishi had told the other Nagas about it. Karishi would be furious if he knew what Kanvar was doing. But what choice did he have but to take the gems from the hall. Consigning a few souls to torment for a time was worth it to keep Khalid from enslaving the world. Wasn't it? Guilt plagued Kanvar.

"I doubt the king has sent us to Darvat for a social visit," Lord Theodoric said. Now he was tense too.

How much should Kanvar tell Lord Theodoric? He was sure Raahi would also want Kanvar to keep the Hall secret. Raahi would be even more furious with Kanvar for desecrating the Hall of his Ancestors than Karishi would. Raahi had sworn an oath to protect it.

Land came into view while Kanvar wrestled with how he could convince his friend to willingly show him to the Hall and let him take the gems from its walls. Towering mountains like jagged spires reached to the sky. In sheer defiance of the rugged terrain, bushes and trees clung like an emerald blanket to the near-vertical slopes. Ishayu approached the mainland from the southwest, and the sun was on its last slide below the horizon. Long shadows, cast by the mountain peaks, knifed across the ground. The scent of greenery wafted to him on the wind.

"You're not going to tell me?" Lord Theodoric said. The disbelief in his voice was tinged with anger.

"My Lord, I'm sorry. I can't. Not yet. I have to get my friend's permission first."

"Your friend's permission is more important than your father's orders?"

Kanvar and Lord Theodoric had spoken little to each other throughout the day as Ishayu had flown them across Varna and out over the water. Kanvar wished they could continue their journey in silence. "My father put me in charge, not you. I'll tell you what we're doing when I'm ready and not before."

"We've reached Darvat. You have to at least tell Ishayu where to fly." Lord Theodoric gripped his sword.

Kanvar did not like flying with Theodoric pressed so close against his back. His father may have told Theodoric to obey Kanvar's orders, but that didn't mean Theodoric would do it.

"If we follow the western coast, we'll reach Huayna, the Darvat capital. There's a river that flows from there up into the heart of the mountains. We need to avoid Huayna but follow the river until I can find my friend's mind. I know he lives in a village somewhere in the mountains along the river, but I don't know which one." Kanvar hoped he would have no trouble recognizing Raahi's mind amid so many other Darvaties.

"Fly up a river into those mountains?" Lord Theodoric shook his head. "It's getting dark. Great Blue dragons may have keen eyesight in the dark, but Great Gold's do not. It's too dangerous to try to fly that tonight. We'll have to wait until morning."

"We can't wait until morning. Your men could be only minutes behind us."

"I don't feel them."

"They'll be shielding their minds. I know it's hard to fly in the dark and dangerous in mountains like these, but we have to try."

Ishayu growled.

"If those are your orders, Your Highness, then we will do it, but note that I advise against it. My men would not choose to fly these mountains in the dark any more than I would. Ishayu is tired. I advise you land now and take up the search for your friend in the morning."

Kanvar gritted his teeth and sent his mind out searching for Raahi's. Huayna had not yet come into sight, but a dizzying array of thoughts and emotions sprang into Kanvar's mind from Huayna and the Darvati villages. Kanvar could not pick Raahi's thoughts out from any of the other humans' thoughts. The more he struggled against the tide of minds, the more disoriented he became. The land below them grew dark and the mountains reached up toward him like raptor claws. He relived the impact and crunch of pain as Dharanidhar had flown straight into a cliff face when first blinded. His wing had broken. Kanvar's arm began to ache where the break had been. Like hot fire, the pain burned down his arm as if he were carrying some heavy load, flapping hard to stay up and move across the sky. His mind swam with the medicine that was supposed to kill the pain. Usually it worked. But not like this. Not with such a heavy load. Kanvar gasped as he realized his mind had slipped into Dharanidhar's. *Dharanidhar, land. Land now before you injure yourself again.*

Dharanidhar snorted in Kanvar's mind. *Not yet. Too many lives at stake.*

But it's dark. So dark. Dharanidhar, please.

It's not dark here yet, Kanvar. If it's dark where you are then land and fly again when it's safe.

I have to get the gems. Kanvar rubbed his arm, trying to ease the pain.

If you can't fly, Khalid's men can't fly either. Land now and wait for dawn.

Dharanidhar's words eased some of the tension in Kanvar's chest. He breathed a bit easier. "My Lord. You're right. We should land," he told Lord Theodoric.

Where, Ishayu asked.

Kanvar shook his head. "I don't know. I can't find Raahi. I don't think we're close enough. Last time we flew here, Dharanidhar landed at a lake, but I don't see it. We must have come to shore in a different place."

Ishayu banked to the left to avoid a peak and then snapped back to the right to avoid another as he eased toward the ground.

"A little moonlight might be nice," Lord Theodoric muttered.

Ishayu dropped down into a ravine and flew past mountains on both sides in the deepening darkness. Kanvar squinted below, looking for any place to land.

"There. I see a pool of water and an open place in the trees," Lord Theodoric said.

Ishayu winged toward it. When they got closer, Kanvar saw it was a rock field along the side of one of the mountains. Worn by weather, the rocks had broken off from the mountain and slid down, partially blocking a stream. Ishayu settled to the ground next to the pool created by the rock fall. He let out a heavy sigh, rolled his shoulders to loosen his wing muscles, then bent down so Lord Theodoric and Kanvar could dismount.

A muffled cry of surprise went up from the far side of the water. A human cry. Someone had seen them. Plants rustled as the person raced away, or tried to. He wasn't moving very fast.

"Wait," Lord Theodoric called.

The rustling of movement continued.

"We probably frightened him." Kanvar reached his mind out to find out if the man had seen Kanvar and Theodoric and figured they were Nagas. He felt a thick shield around the man's mind, trained and powerful. "My Lord, he's a Naga," Kanvar exclaimed.

"Yes, I felt that." A frown creased Theodoric's face.

"One of your men? How could he have reached Darvat before us?" Kanvar reached for his weapons and cursed. They were still gone.

"LaShawn!" Lord Theodoric bolted across the rocks, splashed through the water, and raced after the retreating man.

Kanvar followed more slowly, unsure of his footing in the dark. How nice it would be to run just once like Lord Theodoric did. Don't be stupid, Kanvar chided himself. He'd given up such dreams back when he was a child in Daro.

A path led from the pool through a stand of trees up to a one-room fieldstone house. Faint candle light gleamed between the slats of a shuttered window. Lord Theodoric pounded on the door. "LaShawn, open up. Don't lock me out. Please, I need to see you."

"Go away," a voice called from inside.

"You can't really think I'd do that?" Theodoric said. "All these years I feared you were dead. Open up."

"I *am* dead."

An uncomfortable feeling told Kanvar this could not be one of Lord Theodoric's men. It could only be his missing son. But why would LaShawn not be happy to see his father?

"Open the door." Lord Theodoric tried to push it open, but it was barred from the inside. When that didn't work, he drew his sword and started hacking away at the wood.

"My Lord." Kanvar grabbed his arm, stopping him. "Wouldn't it be easier to levitate the bar to unlock the door? You're old enough; surely you've mastered the ability."

Lord Theodoric swore under his breath, handed Kanvar the sword, and pressed his palms against the wood. There was a thump from inside as the bar lifted and then dropped to the floor.

"No," LaShawn cried as Theodoric barreled his way in.

Kanvar followed, but Theodoric didn't get more than two steps inside before stopping. LaShawn had backed up against the far wall. He looked much like Theodoric only his hair was longer and he had a scar below his left eye. His right arm was twisted oddly as if it had broken and not healed right.

Lord Theodoric gasped, and Kanvar realized at the same moment as Theodoric that LaShawn had both legs missing below the knees. Mud covered the stumps of his legs where he'd been running on them back from the pool.

Lord Theodoric shook his head in disbelief. No one said anything or moved for a long moment.

Then LaShawn groaned, hobbled over to a mattress stuffed with dry grass that sat on the floor, and sank onto it. He bowed his head, refusing to look at his father.

Lord Theodoric swallowed. "What happened?" he asked in a rough whisper.

"The humans." LaShawn spoke so softly Kanvar could hardly hear him. "Tried to kill me. They had stones that were screaming so loud I couldn't think. They trapped Damodar and me in the palace. We fought. A wall collapsed on me, crushing my legs and arm. Damodar pulled me out and flew as best he could as far as he could. We crashed in the water and were separated. The waves carried me ashore where I was rescued by some villagers. They did what they could for me. My legs . . . they couldn't save."

LaShawn fell silent.

Kanvar gritted his teeth and looked down at his own twisted leg, ashamed suddenly that he'd been so frustrated with it. At least he had one good leg to stand on.

"Where's Damodar?" Theodoric moved further into the room so Kanvar could get in.

Kanvar figured Damodar had to be LaShawn's dragon, but the room was too small for a full-sized gold dragon. The roof hung low, barely tall enough to clear Kanvar's head. The floor was dirt. A rough-made stool sat next to the table, which was lower than a regular one. Other than that and the bed, there was no furniture in the house. A hole in the roof at the opposite side from the bed opened up above a small fire pit. No fire burned at the moment, but a single pot hung over the pit. A dented plate and tin cup sat beside it. The room smelled of smoke and sweat.

Kanvar closed the door behind him and lifted the bar back in place.

"He lives on the hill behind this cabin. There's a cave. He can't fly, hasn't since we crashed here. But even if he could—" LaShawn lifted his head to look his father in the eyes for the first time, "—you know we could never come home. Not like this."

Lord Theodoric gave a shaky nod.

"Why not?" Kanvar demanded. "It's not like you were born crippled."

Both Lord Theodoric and LaShawn winced at his blunt use of the word crippled. Lord Theodoric lifted his hand to silence him. "Quiet, Kanvar. You know nothing about Aesir and the Nagas who live there."

LaShawn lifted his gaze to Kanvar. As with every other person when they first saw Kanvar, LaShawn's gaze moved from Kanvar's face down to his stumpy left arm and rested there for a long moment before dropping to his twisted foot. But instead of looking away at that point like most people did, LaShawn snapped his attention back to Kanvar's face. He thought *cripple* and *abomination* forcefully enough Kanvar heard them through LaShawn's shields. But LaShawn's disgust at seeing Kanvar turned quickly back on himself. He was no better. He should be dead as well. But he'd lived. The face of a Darvati woman flashed through LaShawn's mind before LaShawn regained control of his thoughts and locked them away. LaShawn dropped his gaze down to his own crippled body. "I'm sorry, Father."

"But you're alive," Lord Theodoric said. "You're alive." He crossed the room, dropped to his knees and embraced his son. "By the fountain, you're alive. I could not have hoped for a greater thing in all the world."

Kanvar looked away and fiddled with Lord Theodoric's sword. Kanvar's own father had been just as pleased to see Kanvar after their separation too.

LaShawn cleared his throat. "How fares my mother and sisters?"

"They are well. I left them in Garron's care. You have a younger brother. I named him Shaunty in your memory."

LaShawn smiled at the thought of a little brother, but the smile faded quickly. "If Garron is at Aesir, then you brought Captain Vitra with you?" LaShawn frowned at the door as if he expected Captain Vitra to come barging through as well.

"Vitra is . . . not with me at the moment."

"I should think not, or your companion here would surely be dead. How can you tolerate him?" The question was asked about Kanvar, but Kanvar felt LaShawn was really asking, how can you tolerate me? How can you bare to touch me?

Lord Theodoric stepped away from LaShawn and took a seat on the stool. "LaShawn, this is Kanvar, son of Amar the grandson of Khalid, King of Stonefountain. His Majesty ordered me and Ishayu to fly Kanvar here on a vital mission and to obey his commands as if they came from the king himself."

LaShawn rose to his knees and bowed. "Forgive me, Your Highness, but you are . . . a cripple."

Kanvar grinned and handed Lord Theodoric his sword. "Yes, I am. And my father has abolished the law that crippled babies should be killed."

"Not left alive to *suffer*," LaShawn said. "What kind of a life would they have? How cruel it would be to let them die a slow tormented death when the fever comes upon them. Has His Majesty no sympathy?"

"That's how you justify murdering infants, is it?" It was a good thing Kanvar had just given Theodoric the sword. Still, Kanvar thought about punching LaShawn in the face.

LaShawn glared up at him. "You know you can never bond. It would cripple the dragon."

A laugh burst out of Kanvar before he could hold it back. He laughed hard enough water trickled from his eyes. "You'd better not say anything like that to Dharanidhar," Kanvar choked out. "He'll roast you alive."

"Dharanidhar, that's a dragon name. You haven't bonded, have you?"

"Oh, I've bonded," Kanvar said. "And you're lucky Dharanidhar isn't here with me. He has a bit of a temper."

"A temper to match your own," Lord Theodoric said. "Now stop arguing, both of you. LaShawn, Kanvar's bond with his dragon has proved two things that will change our world forever. First, any imperfection either Naga or dragon have before the bonding is not passed on when they share their blood. Second, Nagas are fully capable of bonding with Great dragons other than Golds with no harm to the Naga or dragon. Dharanidhar is a Great Blue dragon and the most unlikely companion any Naga would consider."

"Dharanidhar is the most perfect companion any Naga could have," Kanvar snapped.

"I can't believe it," LaShawn said.

"Believe." Kanvar's stomach grumbled. Too bad there was no food in the house and he didn't have his crossbow to go hunt for some.

"I mean, I can't believe an heir to the throne survived. We have a king. Father, the king lives? And he's changed the laws?"

"Yes." Lord Theodoric slipped his crossbow harness off and handed it to Kanvar. "Good idea. Get us something to eat, Kanvar. LaShawn and I have much to discuss."

Kanvar took the weapon and left the cabin, eager to find something for dinner. Just as the door was closing behind him, he heard LaShawn say, "Can he even use a crossbow?" and Lord Theodoric answer, "I'm pretty sure he can."

Kanvar grinned.

Chapter Twelve

Amar heaved a sigh of relief when Dharanidhar set the platform down on the cliff above the village and released the net he'd been holding with his foreclaws. Dharanidhar had refused to even try to carry the load with his back legs, which on a younger dragon would have been stronger. From Bensharie's back, Amar had been watching the blue dragon fly, watching every flap of his wings become more labored, and worried that the platform with all its precious occupants, including Silverwave who had wound herself around the outside of the net, would slip from Dharanidhar's claws and plummet to the ground. The flight had been precarious, and Amar was glad to see it over. Bensharie set down Aadi, who he'd been carrying in a net by his own hind legs, and landed beside the platform. Frost flapped down from Dharanidhar's shoulder to join them

Dharanidhar lifted Kumar Raza and Chandran from his neck and set them on the ledge, then flapped up to perch on a higher ledge since there wasn't room for him below.

Are you all right? Amar asked Dharanidhar while dismounting.

Dharanidhar let out a low growl. *I still need to carry Silverwave to the coast. She's been out of the water too long already. Just give me a moment to catch my breath.*

It was true. Silverwave was doing about as well out of the water as Frost was in the jungle heat.

Rajan got himself untangled from the net first. Miki barked as he bounded out beside him, but Rajan silenced the dog with a flick of his mind and strode over to the head of the stairs leading down to the village. The village was not readily viewable from the ledge. The steep stairs that had been carved in the volcanic stone wound around the side of the mountain then switched back and forth a few times before dropping below the canopy to the tree platforms where the villagers had built their huts.

"Rajan," Amar warned, moving to stop him.

Rajan put a finger to his lips. *Quiet, Your Majesty. I'm just going around the bend to stand guard. I'll leave the dragon hunters alone unless they come up here.*

"It's a compromise," Kumar Raza whispered. "I suggest you agree to it, Amar."

Amar walked over to Rajan so he could talk quietly. "I don't want you doing anything to their minds. No matter what."

Rajan gave Amar a flat look as if Amar was jabbering nonsense. Rajan lifted a hand and Kumar Raza tossed his sheathed sword into it. Rajan jerked the sword free of its sheath and held the blade up in front of Amar's face. "If they come, would you rather I kill them or send them gently off to bed? One way or another, I won't let them hurt our families."

Amar opened his mouth to argue, but General Chandran grabbed his arm. "Rajan's right. Let him do what he has to do to guard our backs." Chandran leveled a scowl at Rajan. "Just don't do any permanent damage to their minds."

Rajan nodded then hurried down the steps around the side of the mountain.

Amar pulled away from Chandran's grip. "You agree to this? Rajan scares me. I don't know what he's fully capable of."

"He scares me too," General Chandran said. "But I've agreed to join you. If we're going to fight, we need to use whatever resources we have. I agree with you that we should not force the dragon hunters to join us in battle, but there are ten of them, and if we fight them now there won't be any of us left to stop Khalid. If Rajan needs to use his power to keep the dragon hunters out of the way, so be it." Chandran nodded toward the mountain. "Karishi's in there somewhere? How do we get him to open up and let us in? The sooner we get off this ledge, the better."

Amar walked back to the women and took Mani in his arms. He'd had so little chance to hold her for so long.

How precious she was to him. He kissed the top of her head and rested his cheek on her silky hair which somehow always smelled like orchids. Closing his eyes, he reached out to Karishi and found him deep inside the mountain.

Your Majesty, Karishi said, startled. *You're free.*

Miraculously, yes.

Karishi's mind grew agitated. *Tana came to me talking about freeing you, but I couldn't. I don't know why there is such conflict in the palace, but I want no part of it. Is that cowardice? I'm sorry. I should have listened to her, should have come to help you.* Karishi's mind was rife with guilt and confusion. He had not known what side he should take, and had chosen, therefore, to take none. *Are you angry I would not help her? Where is Tana?*

Tana will be here any moment. I'm on the ledge above the village and her dragon is climbing the cliff now. Karishi, I'm not angry with you. I respect your choice to avoid conflict. In a quick mental exchange, Amar shared the present situation with Karishi. *All your life you've guarded the spirits of the dead. Now I need you to guard the living. Come get the women and children and take them into your safe place.*

Relief flooded through Karishi. *You don't want me to fight Khalid?*

No, I want you to stay right here where you're happy.

All right. I'll open a way in from where you are. It will take a minute. Move everyone back from the rock face.

Carrying Tana in her tail and her three wyrmlings on her back, Vasanti slid onto the ledge and set Tana down.

With her added to the group, there wasn't much room for anyone to stand away from cliff, but Amar motioned them back. Everyone edged away, keeping a good distance between themselves and Vasanti.

With a quiet groan, Dharanidhar lifted off from the cliffs, swooped down, and grabbed Silverwave up with his hind legs. To make it easier, Silverwave wrapped her long serpent body around his legs and tightened her coils to hold on.

I'll be back, Dharanidhar said, then flew off toward the coast. That left a bit more space, which was good because the mountain groaned and rocks shook loose and rained down as the cliff face cracked open with a bone-shivering rasp. The resulting opening was only big enough for a human to slip into by turning sideways. Karishi stepped out, his copper scale armor dusted with black from the splitting rocks.

Seeing Vasanti and Bensharie, Karishi pressed his hands to either side of the crack and closed his eyes. The rock twisted outward, the grind and scrape of it loud in the evening air. There was no way the dragon hunters could have missed the sound of the mountain tearing open so that even Vasanti could slither in.

Kumar Raza drew his crossbow, loaded it and headed for the stairs in case his brother needed back up.

Karishi motioned for everyone else to follow him into the mountain.

Amar moved first, leading Mani past Karishi into the gap. "It's good to see you," he whispered to Karishi as he passed. Inside was a narrow, rock-strewn tunnel lit by a torch Karishi had set on the ground while he opened the mountain. Amar picked up the torch and moved deeper in so the others could come behind him.

Keep going until you reach the maze, Karishi said. *I'll close the mountain behind us as soon as Kumar Raza and his brother get back up here.*

"I don't like this," Mani said, clinging to Amar's hand as they followed the tunnel at a steep angle downward. "I can't breathe. We'll be trapped and die."

"You can breathe," Amar reassured her. "There must be fresh air or the torch would go out."

Her fingers tightened on his arm. "I think I should have stayed in Daro."

"You weren't happy in Daro. And the palace was nice. You have to admit that." Amar had not liked the years he'd been separated from her. What good was a comfortable palace without a woman to share it with?

"I wish my father would have warned me I was marrying a Naga," Mani said.

"Would you still have married me?" Amar asked.

"Of course I would not have. Nagas are evil."

Amar stopped and drew back from his wife. "You think I'm evil?"

"Khalid is evil. Rajahansa turned evil along with Haidar and Liander. I don't like being mixed up in all this." Mani's face was stark light and shadow in the flickering flame.

Amar's hand tightened on the handle of the torch. "I'm sorry they hurt you. I love you, Mani. I don't want to lose you."

Mani reached out and rested a hand on his chest. "They hurt you more. And, the fountain help me, I love you too."

Amar leaned down and kissed her, softly and gently. The mountain rumbled as Karishi closed it behind them. *Keep moving*, Karishi urged him. Amar took Mani by the hand and led her deeper into the mountain until they came to a jagged chamber that split into three ways. He supposed this was the maze Karishi had spoken of. He and Mani waited as the others came in behind him.

"Which way? Which tunnel do we go down?" Kumar Raza asked.

Amar was relieved to see there was no blood on Kumar's or Rajan's clothes and weapons. Either the dragon hunters had not come up the steps, or—Amar grimaced—Rajan had done something to their minds.

Karishi brushed past the rest of the group to Amar's side. "None of them. Believe me, you don't want to go down any of these three. Sensing so many unknown and hostile Nagas up there, I created a bit of a safety cushion just in case they've mastered manipulation. Stand back around the edges."

When everyone had cleared the center of the chamber, Karishi knelt and pressed his hands against the floor. Sand and loose rocks clattered as an opening appeared. Tazeran's copper head slid up from the gap, and he flicked his tongue out in greeting.

This is a good mountain, he hissed. *Plenty of tasty rocks and minerals, and no one yelling at me not to eat them.*

"Licking the gold off the walls of someone else's home is not polite," Karishi chided. "I suppose there are still bare patches at the palace?" he said to Amar.

"I'm sure there are," Amar said with a laugh. "I certainly haven't had time to repair them."

"Go on down." Karishi motioned Tazeran out of the way. "There are stairs. Watch your step. They're steep."

Amar continued down. The stairs ended in a complex of connected chambers. The sound of water trickling came from somewhere close by. It wasn't the water that surprised him, though, it was the sunlight. He stepped into the central chamber and found a smooth floor of polished marble illuminated by a shaft of sunlight from overhead. A stone table, scattered with rock and metal objects in various states of completion took up most of the space in the room. Amar blinked up at the light.

Karishi took the torch from him and set it in a sconce on the wall. "Air, light, and water, the three most important things underground. But I know how to architect a home in a mountain. I've had plenty of time to learn." Amar caught a flow of bitter memories from Karishi. He'd been abandoned on a mountainside as a newborn and never knew his father or mother. Some villagers had found him and raised him, treating him as a burden they'd rather not have to bear. He'd lived with their abuses until he'd run away at the age of ten and found a cave to call home. Since then, he'd avoided people as much as possible. Karishi shared the memories with Amar, hoping he would understand why Karishi had let his fear and indecision keep him from helping Tana.

Amar gave him a reassuring thump on the back. "This place is nice, but will there be food for the baby dragons? They'll need meat."

"There's an underground lake with fish. I've stored fruits and nuts from the jungle as well, but the dragons can live on fish."

I love fish, Frost piped up.

"We're not staying here, Frost," Denali said. "We need to go with my father to help fight the Nagas."

Amar cleared his throat and shot a questioning look at Kumar Raza. Denali and Frost would be killed if they joined in the battle. Odds were everyone would be killed and only those left in the mountain would stay free from Khalid.

"Denali." Kumar Raza put a firm hand on Denali's shoulder. "You are a man by Tuniit law, and I need you to do a man's job. I'm counting on you, Denali. I have no one else to turn to."

"You know I'll fight alongside you," Denali said. "Frost and I won't let you down."

Eska's face went pale. "Kumar, please."

"I do need you to fight, Denali." Kumar tapped the hunting knife Denali kept at his waist, the knife he'd used to fight off a ravenous pack of snow wolves. "But I need you to do it here. Someone has to stay and protect the women and children. Karishi has no training with a weapon and no experience in battle. Neither does Aadi. If we fail, if we're killed, you'll be the only man left who can defend our families. I know you want to come to the Maran Colony with me, but your work here is more important. Can I count on you?"

Denali's hand curled around the hilt of the hunting knife. "Frost and I won't let you down. But I don't think you'll be killed. You're too good of a fighter for that."

Kumar Raza grinned, and Amar let out a sigh of relief. He did not want to take Denali into battle with him.

Aadi stepped out of the shadows by the entrance. "You mean for me to stay here as well?"

Amar felt an intense longing reach out from the boy, searching for a dragon, frightened of the emptiness inside him. *There are no dragons here*, Aadi said so only Amar could hear him. *I am alone. I don't know how long I can stand it.*

You lived for many years at the palace and spent time with all the young dragons. Tell me the names of the golds you would choose from, and I'll do everything in my power to free them from Khalid and bring them here. You do not yet have a fever, so there is time.

I wish I did have the fever. I can't stand waiting any longer. I hurt, Your Majesty. Ever since—the memory of the ointment burning into his skin and Rajahansa's gold encircling him, rubbing against his body, flashed through Aadi's mind. For a few minutes he had felt so alive, so full of power, so dazzled by the promised connection to the Great Gold dragon. Then it had been torn from him, leaving a jagged emptiness that grew stronger with time instead of fading. *I'm dying, Your Majesty. I don't have a fever, and I'm dying. I fear I will never get the fever. The ointment has changed me. I can't bond, and I can't live without bonding.*

Aadi's words shook Amar to the center of his heart. A dark fear took him that Aadi might be right. From somewhere that felt like far off, he heard Karishi talking, directing the women to a chamber where they would be comfortable.

"You and Aadi can share that room over there," Karishi said to Denali. "Frost should be fine with you. It's cooler down here than in the jungle, and even cooler by the underground lake. I'll make a nest for your wyrmling's, Vasanti."

You might be wrong, Amar forced himself to tell Aadi. *There is no reason to think you won't come down with the fever any day now. Tell me the names of the dragons you favor, and I'll find them and bring them here for your Choosing Ceremony. If you don't have a fever by then, perhaps we will try the bonding anyway. I know you're a Naga. There's no reason you shouldn't be able to bond.*

You won't find any of the gold dragons. They've all gone to Stonefountain, Aadi's thoughts were bitter and desperate.

"Your Majesty." Karishi addressed Amar, but his mind did not register Karishi's words until he had repeated them several times.

"What?" Amar broke off his conversation with Aadi.

Aadi frowned and slipped away into the room where Denali had gone.

"Your Majesty," Karishi said again. "Please come this way. I need to show you something."

Chapter Thirteen

Amar followed Karishi into another chamber, smaller than the first and dimmer. General Chandran, Kumar Raza, Rajan, and Tana came in behind him. Vasanti stuck her head in. This room was also scattered with various rock and metal items, but these were finished.

Kumar Raza crossed the room and hefted an iron spear from a bundle of them that leaned against the wall. He spun the spear in his hand. "It's a good weight, well balanced, sharp head, but it's iron. Can't you make steel?"

"Oh, I can make steel," Karishi said, lifting a set of gold armor from the chest. "This for instance, is steel like you've never seen made by the best of the Darvati crafts-man. It's stronger and lighter than any forge can produce. The gold covering is not necessary, but I thought it would suit His Majesty better."

He handed the breastplate to Amar, who took it gingerly, expecting it to be heavy, but it was lighter than any steel armor had a right to be. Amar grinned and glanced at the others. Tana rubbed the green dragonhide armor that had once belonged to him. She looked good in it, and Amar had given it to her so she wouldn't be paralyzed by her dragon's poison. She had his crossbow strapped to her back and one of the pair of his jungle knives at her waist. Amar smiled at Tana to reassure her he wanted her to have the armor and weapons.

"I've been working on this set of armor for you since I came to Kundiland," Karishi said to Amar. His face colored. "I never intended for you to need it, mind. I just wanted to make you a present and couldn't think of anything else you didn't already have."

"Thank you." Amar slid into the armor and found that the gold platemail was segmented like the plates of a gold dragon so that even though it covered him completely from the neck down, he could move without obstruction.

"There's a helm too, if you want it." Karishi lifted the last piece out of the box and gave it to Amar.

"So why iron?" Kumar Raza had picked up several of the spears, examining each for craftsmanship. "You said you had spears for me. Why make them like this?"

"I've been thinking." Karishi went to a rectangular iron box that stood against the wall looking ominously like a coffin. He opened it, and the lid swung to the side on well-oiled hinges. "The singing stones hold the spirits of those who once lived at Stonefountain, but their power is blocked inside the iron boxes. If it's true that Naga power also derives from Stonefountain then . . . well, I did a little experiment."

Karishi put down all mental shields and linked minds with Amar in a link so strong it made Amar nervous. He did not like his mind to be that close to anyone else's, not even his dragon's since Rajahansa had turned against him. Karishi gave him a grim smile, stepped into the box, and pulled the lid shut.

The link between them snapped.

Amar gasped and rubbed his head. He could no longer feel Karishi at all. It was as if Karishi had died the instant the box shut.

Tazeran hissed, slid over to the box, and pawed at it until Karishi let himself back out.

Kumar Raza frowned. "What just happened?"

"T-the box," Amar said. "It killed him, I mean...It felt like he was dead, gone, his mind, heart, and soul vanished. I think I'm going to be sick."

Rajan swore and pressed his hand to his heart. "I don't like iron. It hurts. It still hurts. Even now I can feel it, just being close to those spears and that horrible box." Rajan wavered and leaned up against the wall.

Kumar Raza set down the spear and crossed to his brother. "I used iron harpoons to kill the red dragon Rajan was bound to." He put a steadying hand on Rajan's arm.

"It's a wonder he survived. Watch." Karishi grabbed a spear and nicked the back of his hand with it. The wound was small, but the skin around the edges shriveled and turned black as if it had been left untreated for some time and given over to infection.

Karishi grimaced. "Vasanti, will you lick this please?" He walked over to the dragon and held his hand out. "This is something I haven't had a chance to test yet. Metal dragon saliva is not something you want on your skin. No offense Tazeran, but your saliva is so acidic it could eat through anything except your own metal hide."

Tazeran hissed and stuck out his tongue to lick at the matching wound that had manifested on his foreclaw. The wound on Tazeran's foreclaw closed over, but the one on Karishi's hand remained.

"It can't be," Amar said. "If Tazaran's wound heals, yours should heal as well."

"Interesting, isn't it," Karishi said. "Vasanti, let's see if we can do anything with this on my end."

Amar watched while Vasanti licked Karishi's hand. The wound remained open.

Rajan shuddered. Kumar Raza swore under his breath and glanced over at Chandran. Chandran's face was grim, but a fierce light came into his eyes.

Karishi shook his head, pulled a clean strip of cloth from the chest, and wound it around his hand. "Nasty, isn't it. I've been nicked with iron before. It happens often enough with the work I do. I didn't realize it wasn't normal until I came here and saw what Great Dragon saliva can do. Takes a week or two to heal."

"I don't understand the point of this," Amar said.

"I felt a lot of Nagas out there," Karishi said. "They didn't seem friendly. Human soldiers could never get inside this mountain. But Nagas could. They could feel me. They could manipulate the tunnels open and come after me. They may even get past my traps in the maze. But I knew their dragons wouldn't fit down here. The iron spears are my best defense. I could strike the Nagas, and they would die from their wounds. Not that I want to kill anyone, but I don't want to be killed either. And I saw in their minds how much they despise Nagas not bound to gold dragons. My link to Tazeran is a death sentence by their law. So I fashioned the most deadly weapons I could."

Kumar Raza chuckled. "Karishi, you're brilliant. I've been cut with iron before too. The dragon saliva worked on me, so the problem with iron must be a full-blood Naga thing. That means the spears will be no special use against the soldiers, but the Nagas. Let's set this out plainly so His Majesty can follow. If you hit the Naga with the spear, the wound will show on the dragon like usual. The dragon can lick it closed, but that won't heal the Naga like it usually does. Or in Rajan's case, I hit the dragon with the iron weapon. It showed on Rajan. Silverwave was able to close the wound on Rajan, but that did not heal it on the red dragon."

Rajan's face was pale. "It hurt though."

"Yes, well, any time you get impaled by a whaling harpoon it's going to hurt," Kumar Raza said.

General Chandran crossed the room and picked up two of the spears. When he turned back to face the others, his eyes were cold. Amar backed away, alarmed. Karishi had found a weapon that could kill Nagas like no other.

"Don't try anything." Rajan unsheathed Kumar Raza's sword. "My oath to leave your mind alone is conditional on you not trying to kill us."

General Chandran shook his head. "There are five spears here and five Nagas up there. I'm not going to waste these on you. Karishi, can you make more? Spears, swords, crossbow bolts, all iron?"

Karishi nodded. "It will take time."

"If Kanvar can get the singing stones to free my soldiers' minds, and I can arm my men with iron weapons. Those Nagas won't have a chance. And Khalid . . ." Chandran's grip on the spears tightened so his knuckles went white. "Khalid will fall."

"That's *when* we get the singing stones," Kumar Raza said. "Right now we have a different battle to worry about, one where we're grossly outnumbered and overpowered. One that is going to take stealth, cunning, and surprise. You know the Maran Colony, General. Come draw it out for me, so we can plan. Karishi, do you have paper and ink?"

"I have better," Karishi said, "slate and chalk."

Amar stared at the iron coffin on the far side of the room while the fighters began to plan. The feel of Karishi's mind snapping away from his own still stung. It gave him a strange foreboding, and he didn't want to go anywhere near the coffin or the iron spears.

Kanvar borrowed Theodoric's sword to skin and clean the scaly ibex he'd called down off the rocks and killed with Theodoric's crossbow. He sorely missed his own crossbow. Theodoric's was cumbersome and difficult to handle with Kanvar's stumpy left hand. But that didn't stop him from bagging the ibex for dinner. Outside the cabin, he found a saw and a hatchet for cutting firewood. Too bad Dharanidhar wasn't there to roast the meat for him. A normal fire would have to do. Kanvar cut the wood, hauled it in, and lit a fire then set the ibex to cook over it. He stayed focused on his work, letting the two other men catch up with each other's lives and discuss the current situation.

When dinner was ready, Kanvar cut the sizzling meat off the bones, set it on the tin plate, and took it to Theodoric and LaShawn. Kanvar needed no plate for his food. Living with Dharanidhar, he'd grown comfortable tearing it from the bones with his teeth.

"Thank you," Lord Theodoric said, looking surprised as he took the plate.

Kanvar shrugged. "I'll go get some water to drink and clean up." He grabbed the pot from beside the crackling fire and went down to the pond. It made him sad to think that LaShawn had spent all this time living out here alone with only his dragon for company. Kanvar could not even imagine how lonely that must have been. But LaShawn need not be lonely anymore now that he'd been reunited with his father. Kanvar frowned. He and Theodoric could not stay here with LaShawn. They had to get the singing stones back to Kundiland as quickly as possible. Ishayu might be able to carry all three of them away, but not LaShawn's dragon. If Damodar couldn't fly, LaShawn could not go off to Kundiland and leave him.

Troubled, Kanvar got the water and hauled it back in. By the time he got to the hut, he was winded and sweaty. He stood outside for a moment to catch his breath. From inside he heard LaShawn's remorseful voice. "I didn't mean to fall in love with a human woman, Father. It's just . . . she saved my life. She tended my wounds. She took care of me and we . . . well. I'm sorry, I was weak, and she was beautiful. We loved each other and got married in secret, because her father refused to let her marry a crippled man. When her father found out, he was furious. He legally dissolved our marriage and came to kill me. I only escaped because Damodar came to my aid. But that gave away I was a Naga, and the villagers began to hunt us. We crawled up here and hid and have not gone anywhere near the humans since."

Gritting his teeth, Kanvar pushed his way into the cabin. He didn't want to hear any more of LaShawn's sad life. It wasn't fair. If LaShawn would have flown west to escape from Stonefountain instead of east, he might have crashed in Kundiland where Parmver and Kanvar's father could have seen to his injuries. Parmver might have been able to save his legs. In the very least he would have set his arm correctly so Damodar could fly.

Kanvar set the pot down, dipped out a cup of water, and offered it to Lord Theodoric.

Lord Theodoric took it reluctantly. "Kanvar, you're a prince, an heir to the throne. We should be serving you, not the other way around."

Kanvar snorted. "I spent half my life as an indentured servant. Cooking, hauling, and serving are second nature to me. I would die of boredom if someone did them for me."

When Theodoric finished drinking, Kanvar dipped some water out for LaShawn as well. As he set the cup into LaShawn's good left hand, he stared hard at his crippled right arm, imagining how it could have been set to make it whole and usable. Why hadn't the humans done it right?

"Your Highness, what's done is done," LaShawn said, catching a bit of Kanvar's thoughts.

Kanvar thickened the shields around his mind so his thoughts wouldn't interfere with LaShawn's. "I don't want to leave you here," Kanvar said. "When Lord Theodoric and I leave Darvat, we're taking you with us. I just need to think of a way." Kanvar sat down by the fire and took his armor off to clean it.

Lord Theodoric and LaShawn fell into an awkward silence. But even while Kanvar worked, he couldn't help glancing up to stare at LaShawn's arm.

LaShawn colored, ashamed of his crippled body. "Just leave me, Your Highness. There's nothing you can do, and I will be useless to help in your fight against Khalid."

Kanvar set his armor aside. "You're not useless. You are just temporarily slowed down a bit. I was slow when I was young. I can't tell you how long it took me to learn to walk, to swing a sword, to use a crossbow. Other boys my age had long since mastered everything before I got barely functional at it. But that didn't stop me. I learned to be useful anyway. I'm still slow. Everything takes me longer, but it doesn't stop me, and it doesn't have to stop you."

"It already has stopped me," LaShawn said. "And right now, you don't have time for anyone to slow you down."

"I have until morning." Kanvar got up and paced the small room, trying to think how Parmver would have healed LaShawn's arm.

"Stop," LaShawn said. "Just stop. I can't tell what you're thinking, and I don't like the look on your face."

"I was thinking that I know a Naga who could have fixed your arm. I've watched him heal people before. He was amazing," Kanvar said.

"Was?" Lord Theodoric said.

"Khalid murdered him." Kanvar's heart twinged, feeling the loss at Parmver's passing. Was there any man who deserved to die less than Parmver? Such a patient old man. Kanvar hadn't even given himself a chance to think about Parmver's death until now. "Parmver lived for over a thousand years, and Khalid killed him a few days ago." Anger surged through Kanvar, but he shoved it aside. Anger would not bring Parmver back or help him now.

He balled his hand into a fist and tried to remember all the implements Parmver had down in his lab, tools he'd used to save Kumar Raza's life. There'd been a drill. He'd drilled through Kumar Raza's skull to drain the blood that was pooling on his brain and killing him. Sharp knives for cutting through skin, saws for cutting bone. Parmver's tools had horrified Kanvar at the time, and he'd left the room, unable to watch the procedure. That was then. Kanvar had seen a lot more wounds since. He stopped at the table and picked up the razor. "I think I can fix this. I believe I know what Parmver would do."

Lord Theodoric got to his feet. "The wound healed long ago. There's nothing you can do now?"

"Oh, I think there is." Kanvar pressed the tin cup into Lord Theodoric's hands. "Go get Ishayu to fill this with his saliva."

Lord Theodoric opened his mouth to protest, but Kanvar spoke first. "That's an order, My Lord. Do it."

While Lord Theodoric was gone, Kanvar set the water over the fire to heat it and fetched the hatchet from outside. The saw was too cumbersome to be of any use for Kanvar one handed. He washed the hatchet and razor in the hot water, making sure they were clean of rust and dirt that would cause an infection.

LaShawn watched him, lips pressed tightly together, white faced.

"Is that blanket on your bed the only cloth you have?" Kanvar asked. The blanket was ratty and old. Kanvar had seen better fabric on untouchables in Daro.

"You think I could spin and weave anything useful?" LaShawn snapped. "Of course it's all I have. I told you, I stay away from the humans. That blanket's the best I could make."

"I meant no offense." Kanvar cleared off the table except for the razor and the hatchet. Then he took off his shirt and cut it up to make a cloth for washing and strips for bandages. If all went well, he wouldn't need the bandages, but there would certainly be a mess to clean up after.

Lord Theodoric returned with the dragon saliva and surveyed Kanvar's perpetrations. "I don't like this."

"Don't worry. LaShawn won't feel anything, I promise." Kanvar had succeeded in blocking Tana's pain when he cut her for the Bonding Ceremony. This would be the same, though it would probably take a bit more concentration. The biggest problem would be convincing LaShawn to go along with it and hold still.

LaShawn glared at him. "How old are you exactly? Fifteen? Sixteen? You think you can do surgery like a trained Aesir healer? There is no way I'm going to let you cut into me."

"I'm almost seventeen. But I bet I've done more in my seventeen years than you have in a hundred." Kanvar took the cup of saliva from Lord Theodoric and set it on the table next to the razor.

"I highly doubt that," LaShawn said.

"When I was ten, I survived an attempted poisoning and escaped someone trying to shoot me with a crossbow. Despite being hunted by dragon hunters I got myself from Varna to Maran and from there to Kundiland. When I was fifteen I faced an enormous Great Blue dragon with only a sword, blinded him and escaped. I stood down a rampaging Great Green dragon with a crossbow and only one bolt. I fought a battle to the death with another Great Blue dragon. I traveled to the Great North and rescued my grandfather from a volcano. Then made another trip here to Darvat to help my friend, Raahi, free his country from Maran slavery. I got caught in a hurricane, crash landed in the ocean, survived to return home and—"

"I think that's enough," Lord Theodoric said.

"I'm just getting started. I haven't even talked about stopping a rogue Naga from taking over the world or facing a Great Red volcanic dragon in its lair and helping defeat it."

"Kanvar," Lord Theodoric interrupted him again. "You've said enough, really."

"LaShawn does not look convinced."

"It doesn't matter. I'm convinced. Though I've seldom watched the healers at work, I think I get a feel for what you're intending. I doubt you can do it alone, but the two of us together can make it happen. LaShawn, lie down on the table."

LaShawn shook his head. "I don't want to do this."

"You have nothing to lose," Lord Theodoric said. "I doubt we can make your arm worse, and we may just be able to fix it."

"No." LaShawn hobbled to the door and tried to leave. From outside came the heavy sound of a crippled dragon dragging itself along the ground. "Maybe you can fix my arm, but you can't fix what isn't there. I will not go anywhere with you where people can see me. All my friends in the Naga Guard, all the . . . girls that I grew up with in Aesir, I want them to remember me the way I was: strong and powerful, the son and heir of the ruler of Navgarod. I will not have them ever know that I lived one day of my life as a cripple."

"To the fountain with your pride." Kanvar lunged across the room, grabbed the front of LaShawn's shirt with his right hand, dragged him over to the table, and slammed him down on his back. "That's what this is all about? You don't want anyone to see you like this? Frankly, I don't care what you want. I don't know how many Nagas there are in Navgarod, but here only ten have lived to adulthood in a thousand years. Of those, only six are still alive and one of them, my brother, is lost to us. Every Naga life is precious, including yours, whether you want it to be or not."

"Let me go." LaShawn struggled to get out of Kanvar's grip.

"Be still." Kanvar stabbed his way through LaShawn's shields and took control of his body, freezing his muscles so he could not move.

LaShawn's eyes went wide. He tried to fight Kanvar with his own power, but it was no match for the strength Kanvar drew from Dharanidhar even at a distance, though Dharanidhar gasped in the back of Kanvar's mind and swooped down to land in the blue dragon cove on the Kundiland coast. Silverwave uncurled herself from Dharanidhar and slithered into the water.

Warn me next time, Dharanidhar muttered. He was tired and aching, but he leant all the strength he could to Kanvar. It far outweighed the trickle of feeble power LaShawn drew from his dragon. Both had been sedentary for far too long.

Lord Theodoric grabbed Kanvar's arm. "Let him go. We can't do this. Not with him fighting us."

"Back off. That's an order," Kanvar said.

Lord Theodoric clenched his fists and stepped away.

Kanvar took a deep breath to get control of his temper. Pride was a luxury he'd never had. He let go of LaShawn but kept him pinned on the table as he picked up the razor. "Turn away." He forced LaShawn's head to turn so he couldn't see Kanvar work.

"My Lord," Kanvar said. "Do you know how to block a person's pain?"

"I . . . that's what healers are for."

Kanvar let out a bitter laugh. "So much power and completely helpless. You should spend some time as a servant, My Lord. It would be good for you." Kanvar reached over and pinched LaShawn's arm so he could pinpoint the pain centers associated with it in LaShawn's mind. LaShawn gritted his teeth as Kanvar got control of that part of his mind as well and blacked all feeling from his arm.

"Do not interrupt me," Kanvar told Lord Theodoric. "If you break my concentration, this is really going to hurt."

He felt down LaShawn's arm until he found where it had been broken and set wrong before. Using the razor, he sliced the flesh open to the bone and stopped the spurt of blood with a lick of saliva on the open flesh. Then came the part Kanvar wasn't sure he could do well with the tools he had. He had to re-break the bone in a way that it could be adjusted properly and reset. His stomach twisted as he tapped the healed-over spot on the bone with the hatchet. Nothing happened. He'd have to hit it harder. Wincing, he slammed the hatchet against the bone. There was a crunching sound, and the bone split in several directions none of them the one Kanvar had intended.

Lord Theodoric muttered a swear word under his breath.

"What's going on? Let me go." LaShawn started fighting Kanvar again.

"No. Hold still." Lord Theodoric rushed to the table and held his son in place, quieting his mind. "Try it again, Kanvar. You can't stop now. You've gone too far."

Cringing, Kanvar tapped the bone again and managed to get a break along the line he needed. He set down the hatchet and tried to manipulate the bone into the correct place, but couldn't get the pieces to go right one handed.

"I told you you'd need my help," Lord Theodoric said. "Do I have your permission, Highness."

"Yes. Do it." Kanvar moved his hand so Lord Theodoric could realign the bone the way it should have been set when first broken. While he worked, Kanvar kept a firm grip on LaShawn's mind so he would not move and he felt no pain.

Once the bone was aligned, Kanvar spread the dragon saliva directly on it, letting it seep in and heal the fractures Kanvar had made. Then he closed the wound, bit-by-bit, applying dragon saliva over each layer of muscle and skin while Lord Theodoric held it in place. When they were finished, LaShawn had a wide red scar, but his arm lay at a natural angle.

Kanvar eased back his control of LaShawn's mind. "I think it will ache for a while," he said, thinking of

Dharanidhar's legs and wings. The ache had never quite left those completely, but Dharanidhar was much older than LaShawn. Wetting the cloth he'd made from his shirt, Kanvar wiped the blood from LaShawn's arm and table.

Groaning, LaShawn rolled off the table. Lord Theodoric helped him over to the bed while Kanvar finished cleaning up.

"In the morning your father and I will be flying upriver. When we return, we'll take you and Damodar with us to Kundiland," Kanvar told LaShawn.

LaShawn rolled on his side with his back to Kanvar and did not respond.

"I'm going out to check on Damodar." Theodoric said. "We can't be sure that fixing LaShawn's arm will have healed Damodar's wing completely as well."

Kanvar let him go. Meticulously, he washed the razor and hatchet and put them away. But his eyes kept straying to his own twisted leg. Could a similar procedure give him what he'd never had before, the ability to walk like a normal man? Parmver had never even suggested it. Why not? What could it hurt to try?

It could hurt me a lot, Dharanidhar rumbled. *They may be able to fix your leg, but what would that do to mine?*

Kanvar shuddered. Dharanidhar was right. Perhaps if the surgery had been done before he bonded. But not now.

While Kanvar was putting his armor on, Lord Theodoric thumped back into the cabin. "I looked at

Damodar's wing. It's weak from lack of use, but it seems to be straight. His forearm is healed as well. It might take a good deal of effort to lift him off the ground. I don't see any way we can take him with us tomorrow."

"I don't like the idea of leaving him here alone. Perhaps Damodar could fly with Ishayu's assistance."

Kanvar, Lord Theodoric spoke into his mind so only he could hear. *You can't force LaShawn to leave his home if he doesn't want to. It would be unkind and unethical to do so. I'm happy enough just knowing he's alive. Give him some time. Let his arm heal. Let Damodar's wings get strong again. When he's ready, I think LaShawn will come to us. If we try to force him to come now, it will only make him hate us.*

"All right." Kanvar said. He went to the door. "I'll be outside waiting for dawn. We need to leave as soon as possible."

Chapter Fourteen

Kanvar woke when the first gray light of morning silhouetted the jagged peaks around him. He'd slept leaning against the cabin, not wanting to be inside with Lord Theodoric and LaShawn. He'd lost his temper and was ashamed of it. He should not have forced the surgery on LaShawn and couldn't sort out why it had been so important to him. Perhaps because there was no way to fix his own crippled arm. Kanvar stared down at it. It ended where most people's elbow would be. Attached was an odd-shaped hand with only two fingers and a thumb.

When he was very young, he hadn't realized he was different from other boys. By the time he was old enough to realize the truth, he already faced the mocking jeers of other dragon hunter children. He'd responded with anger and violence. The other boys soon learned to keep their mouths shut or suffer a beating.

Kanvar flexed his deformed hand. Something about the way LaShawn had acted had triggered Kanvar's fight instinct. It was one thing to punch someone in the face, but another thing to use Naga powers so brutally. He pictured Parmver frowning at him and imagined him saying, *You have to learn to control it, Kanvar. You can't change the world, you can only change yourself. If you abuse your power, you'll be no better than Khalid.*

Kanvar bowed his head in shame. "I'm sorry, Parmver. I suppose I've made an enemy now instead of a friend," he whispered.

"I thought Parmver was dead," Lord Theodoric said.

Kanvar jerked in surprise. He hadn't heard Lord Theodoric slip out the front door.

Catching his breath, Kanvar got to his feet. "My Lord, I . . . is LaShawn very angry at me? I should not have . . . I behaved badly."

Lord Theodoric waved his hand dismissively. "Yes, he's angry, but he's also grateful . . . and confused and ashamed."

"Will he forgive me?" Kanvar glanced at the lightening sky. They'd be able to fly soon.

"You haven't asked his forgiveness."

"Uh." Kanvar smoothed his unruly hair and wiped dirt and twigs from his armor. "Right. Wake Ishayu. We should go now." Kanvar limped over to the door and let himself in the cabin. It was the same as it had been the night before: dark and cold and barren. LaShawn sat on the bed, flexing his right hand and bending the arm up and down at the elbow.

"Does it hurt?" Kanvar asked.

LaShawn looked up, his eyes tight, his face pale. "It aches like you said it would."

"There's medicine for that back in Kundiland. My dragon can't fly without it. He's a little worse for the wear, I'm afraid."

LaShawn's forehead furrowed in a frown, and he said nothing.

Kanvar fidgeted in the awkward silence. "Lord Theodoric says you don't want to come to Kundiland. I've agreed not to force you to come, but I want you to know you'll always be welcome. My father and the other Nagas left alive there will think no less of you for your missing legs. If you only knew my father and understood the kind of man he is . . . but you don't? By the fountain, it took me forever to trust him enough to get to know him."

"He must be a good king." LaShawn's voice was rough and abrupt.

"He is. I, on the other hand, am a very poor son. I behaved badly last night, and I'm sure he would be ashamed of me. I don't blame you if you hate me now, but I want to say I'm sorry and ask you not to judge my father and the other Nagas in Kundiland by my actions." Kanvar swallowed, tense and waiting.

LaShawn clenched his right hand into a fist, then relaxed it and stretched his fingers. "You healed my arm, and you're apologizing for that?"

"I should have waited until you wanted it done. My father is a gentle and patient man and would never have condoned my actions." Kanvar had first encountered such healing methods from his father when Amar healed his leg. In a sense, his father had taken control of Kanvar's mind and body against his will to do it, but that was different. Amar had been loving and gentle. In his mind, he'd been healing a child who did not know any better than to struggle against the healer trying to help him. Kanvar had been angry and brutal in taking control of LaShawn's mind and body. His actions were reprehensible even to himself.

Lord Theodoric stepped into the cabin. "Ishayu's ready. Let's go."

"Just a moment." Kanvar had been equally difficult with Lord Theodoric, refusing to tell him why they'd come to Darvat. The Hall of Ancestors was a dear secret, but Kanvar couldn't keep it from Lord Theodoric. In the end, he had to have Theodoric's help to open up the passage to it, which Karishi had sealed. Kanvar didn't like to think he needed anyone's help. He'd been wrong about that with the surgery. LaShawn could have died if Lord Theodoric had not stepped in to set the bone and help close the wound. Kanvar couldn't risk failure in getting the gems. "My Lord, you can manipulate stone, can't you? My father seemed to take it for granted you could. He knows I have not yet mastered it."

LaShawn snorted. "You're sixteen. You shouldn't even be thinking about trying yet."

Kanvar clenched his fist. He would not let LaShawn get him angry again.

"I have spent very little time manipulating stone in my life," Lord Theodoric said. "That is for the architects and builders to do. However, I have recently been forced to learn the skill." The depth of the regret in Theodoric's voice struck Kanvar. "Unfortunately, I mastered it too late to save my youngest child."

Lord Theodoric had mentioned his daughter had died in an earthquake. "My Lord, I'm sorry," Kanvar said.

"We should go. You said this mission is urgent. We don't have much time." Lord Theodoric held the door open for Kanvar.

"Before we go, I need to explain to you why we're here and what we must do. But first I must have your oath you will not reveal what I tell you to anyone. Both of you." Kanvar looked from father to son. "This touches on a matter sacred to the Darvati people. I have been entrusted with the knowledge only because the guardian of it is my friend and he needed my help to keep it safe."

"You have my oath of secrecy," Lord Theodoric said. "LaShawn?"

"I give my oath," LaShawn agreed.

As quickly as Kanvar could, he explained about the Hall of the Ancestors and the gems on the walls inside that could replace the singing stones and what that meant for their ability to defeat Khalid. "The problem is, I've never been there so I don't know the location. I know only that it is hidden in a mountain somewhere at the head of the River of Death that flows out past Huayna. There was a passage to it, but that has been sealed. Only Raahi can show us how to get there. Then we'll need someone who can reopen the passage."

"We'd better go find your friend then," Lord Theodoric said. "Farewell, LaShawn. I'll come visit you again when the rightful king has regained his throne."

"Farewell, Father." LaShawn got to his knees to clasp his father's hand, an awkward move that brought his head up barely above Lord Theodoric's waist. That did not stop father and son from embracing.

Kanvar stepped outside to let them finish their goodbyes.

Amar watched Rajan pace back and forth across the chamber Karishi had given them to rest for the night. Kumar Raza slept soundly on a mat at the edge of the round chamber. Though his soft snores vibrated the air, his hand twitched on the hilt of his sword, which lay on the mat beside him. He'd spent a long time with Karishi even after General Chandran and Rajan had finished. Though Kumar Raza now slept, Karishi remained awake, working on something in the adjacent room.

General Chandran dozed while sitting with his back against the wall next to one of several stone chests in the room, which Karishi used to store his tools and belongings. Chandran, too, had his sword close by as well as his loaded crossbow.

Rajan had spent some quiet time with Dove alone in the passage down to the underground lake as the daylight slowly vanished from the chambers and Karishi lit more torches. Amar had seen Mani to the women's chamber and held her until she fell asleep before returning to gather with the men.

The women were nervous and upset. How could he blame them? Mani had begged Amar not to fight, but he couldn't give in to her with the lives of the villagers at stake. Through their whole discussion, Denali, Frost, and Miki had played tag around the complex until Eska scolded them and sent them to bed. Aadi had crept off quietly to the lake and not returned. Amar could sense him dangling his feet in the cool water, preferring darkness and solitude to the noise and confusion that radiated from Denali.

Rajan growled as he paced, clenching and unclenching his fists. Amar could not read his mind to see what was troubling him. "You should rest," Amar said quietly so as not to wake the others.

"You're not sleeping either," Rajan said. He kept working his hands and staring around him as if he had lost something and expected to find it somewhere in the room.

"How can I with you this worked up? What's wrong? Don't you like the battle plans Kumar and General Chandran agreed on? You argued less than usual with your brother." Amar settled onto a mat of his own. The room felt stifling with the smell of sweat and metal, though Karishi insisted he'd made sufficient air vents to the surface.

"The plans are sound. I just don't have…Can you believe this place? This mountain was a volcano once, alive and hot. Now it's lifeless and empty." Rajan clenched his fists. "I know, Silverwave. I know."

"What did she say?" Amar kept his voice soft and coaxing. Rajan's agitation concerned him.

"She said she's sorry I can't go home."

"Home to the volcano?"

"Yes, Amar. To the volcano. *My* volcano." Rajan's face flushed and his fists clenched so hard they shook.

"Why go back there? You were a prisoner. I don't imagine the red dragon was nice to you. You showed me your scars."

"I *was* the red dragon. There was no distinction between our minds. As a silver dragon now, I don't relish killing, but if I have to fight tomorrow, I'd prefer not to do it unarmed." He looked down at his hands and spread his fingers like claws.

"We have Karishi's spears."

"Not what I need."

"You want a crossbow?"

"I was never any good with a crossbow."

"A sword?" Amar searched Rajan's troubled face, trying to understand the turmoil.

Rajan shook his head and went back to pacing. "*You* ought to have a sword. You may need it. I want something else."

Amar closed his eyes and pictured his own sword, the golden hilt, the elegant runes that graced the blade, the way the power flowed through him when he held it. The king's sword was familiar to him, and he'd mastered summoning it long ago. Only this time, when he focused his power to bring it to him, the sword did not come. Something blocked it, holding it back from his summoning.

"What are you doing?" Rajan said.

"Trying to summon my sword, but it's not answering my call."

"Wait, you can summon?" Rajan's voice grew intense. "You can bring a sword here into the heart of the mountain?"

"Not just any sword. My sword. Summoning has nothing to do with distance or obstacles in between, it's more like being so much a part of something or it so much a part of you that both parts exist together in a place outside of the material world. And since they are already together in that place, they can be together here. I know that doesn't sound like it makes any sense. There really aren't words to describe it. You just have to feel it." Amar tried again for his sword, and again came up empty handed. Kanvar had carried it last, and there was no reason Amar should not be able to summon it from him. But Kanvar had been a prisoner of Khalid, which meant . . . Khalid had the sword, a sword he himself had forged and imbued with power from Stonefountain. Of course, the sword was more a part of Khalid's existence than Amar's. Amar would never be able to call the sword back from him.

Frowning in irritation, Amar tried for a different weapon instead. During the years he posed as a dragon hunter, he'd carried a pair of jungle knives. He knew those well enough to summon them. One was in the room next door with Tana. The other he'd last seen in Liander's possession. Liander was dead, but the jungle knife must still exist somewhere. He focused his mind and the knife appeared in his hands. It was covered with mud and dead leaves and had started to rust in places as if it had sat for days on the jungle floor. He held it out to Rajan. "It's a good knife, really. Just needs to be cleaned and sharpened."

Rajan stared at him with an unsettling intensity. "The Nagas have swords. The jungle knife is too short to be effective against them. I lost my sword to the Maranies when they captured me in Daro. If you show me how to summon it, I'll give it to you."

He dropped to his knees on the floor in front of Amar. "Take over my mind. Use it to call my sword. Let me see how it's done so I can learn this skill."

"If it's not the sword you want, than what? I can summon the other for you just as well if you let me into your mind." Amar was uncomfortable that close to Rajan and had to force himself to stay put instead of scooting away.

"You don't want to see that part of my mind, Amar. Just summon my sword and I'll be able to get the rest on my own."

"I don't think you should jump to summoning before learning manipulation first. It's not safe." Amar succumbed to instinct and inched away from Rajan.

"Safe? Tomorrow we're going to fight five trained Nagas and a garrison of soldiers You call that safe? If I'm to have any chance against them, I need to do this."

"I can do it for you."

"No, you can't. You will never be connected enough with my weapons, other than the sword, to summon them for me. I'm not a child. I've spent a long time mastering my powers. Just show me how to do it." Rajan's eyes flashed fire, reflecting the torchlight.

Amar shuddered.

"Come on, Amar." Rajan dropped his shields and laid open a way into his mind for Amar to follow.

Amar went cautiously, careful to keep the private parts of his mind separate. Rajan kept his own mind controlled as well, only letting Amar see his memories of the sword. It was a fine sword, one of the best Amar had ever seen. Rajan's father had given it to him when he was young, and he'd practiced with it every day for hours on end until his hands blistered and bled. But he wrapped his hands with bandages and continued to learn. Later, when he'd been alone in the red dragon's lair, he'd continued the daily practice with his sword. He had no one to fight, no dragons to hunt, but the sword was so much a part of him, he could not lay it aside. Rajan's connection to the sword was so strong it was not hard for Amar to focus Rajan's mind to call it to him.

"Yes," Rajan exclaimed as soon as he felt the weight of the sword in his hands. He jumped to his feet. "I see. I understand. It's perfect."

His shout woke General Chandran and Kumar Raza. They both sprang to their feet, weapons in hand.

"Look at this," Rajan said holding up the sword to them. "Isn't it beautiful?"

General Chandran scowled. Kumar Raza smiled. "You still have it?"

"I have it again now, thanks to His Majesty." Rajan whirled back to Amar and held the sword out to him. "Here. You'll need a weapon in battle tomorrow. Those spears are a nasty piece of work, but nothing beats a good sword."

Amar took it hesitantly. "Thank you. Be careful, Rajan. I made that look easy, but it's not."

Rajan turned his back on Amar and spread his hands. The room fell silent. General Chandran opened his mouth to ask what was going on, but Kumar, sensing Rajan's need to focus, motioned for Chandran to be quiet. Moments inched by. Kumar Raza's face lost all color, and he pressed his hand to his head struggling to put up a shield between his mind and his brother's, but whatever Rajan was focusing on seemed to run too deep and powerful for Kumar to block it. Amar wrapped Kumar Raza's mind in his own and blocked it from his brother's.

Sweat slicked Rajan's neck and arms. His hands trembled. Nothing changed, and then . . .

Steel glinted on the back of his forearms and hands. Not in his hands, on the back of them—jointed steel strapped to his forearm, wrist, and hand. The weapons extended four inches past his fingertips in tapered claws, razor sharp. Rajan flexed and curled his hands, and the segmented claws moved with his fingers as if they were a natural part of him—dragon claws fashioned for human use.

General Chandran swore and his face went red in contrast to Kumar Raza's paleness. Amar's stomach felt queasy. He was sure he did not want to know what Rajan had done with those claws while bonded with the red dragon. Rajan turned back to face Amar with a look of triumph on his face.

"By the fountain," Kumar Raza said. "How do you not cut yourself with those?"

"I'm careful not too curl my fingers too tight unless there is something else in the way." Rajan's lips drew back in what was supposed to be a smile but looked more like a snarl to Amar.

Chapter Fifteen

Ishayu winged high over Huayna. Last time Kanvar had been there, fires burned in the streets and the Darvaties, lead by Kumar Raza, had dealt a critical blow to the Maran armies, forcing a treaty that guaranteed Darvati autonomy. Now the city, built on the side of the mountain with its steep stairs and terraces, seemed peaceful. The Darvaties in their colorful wool clothes were out on morning errands undisturbed by war.

"If only it could stay this peaceful," Kanvar said.

"Not likely with it being such a strategic place to Khalid. My men are sure to be right behind us," Lord Theodoric said.

Kanvar clenched his teeth. I should warn Bolivar, he thought. He'll need to gather his army. But without the singing stones, Bolivar's army would fare no better than General Chandran's had. Kanvar had to retrieve the stones first, which meant he had to find Raahi.

The sky was clear and blue. Kanvar was thankful for that. He was less likely to be seen that way. He wondered if it would look strange from the ground to see a ripple of air with a man flying through the sky.

Lord Theodoric chuckled. "They can't see you from directly below. Ishayu's body is between you and their eyes. We can be seen at just the right angle from the side though. The people of Navgarod are used to seeing Nagas, so it wouldn't be a surprise to them. It may be a shock to the people of this city, but we aren't stopping here, are we?"

"Not yet. We need the gems from the Hall first."

"Any sign of your friend?"

Kanvar stretched his mind out in search of Raahi and was once again inundated with the thoughts of Huayna's citizens. The sudden rush gave him a headache. He knew Raahi's mind well, but Raahi felt very much like all the other Darvaties that thronged the city and mountain villages.

"Kanvar," Theodoric said.

Kanvar, once again, rode right in front of him, so Theodoric's legs were pressed against Kanvar's hips and Theodoric's chest was up against Kanvar's back. Uncomfortably close in Kanvar's opinion, and he flinched when Lord Theodoric put a hand on his shoulder. "You have amazing power and ability for one so young, but I get the feeling you haven't spent much time around large crowds of people."

"Great Blue dragons are unfond of people. They prefer seclusion." In the back of Kanvar's mind Dharanidhar chuckled at Kanvar's understatement. He was perched on the cliff ledge above the jungle village, watching the sky for the first hint of coming daylight. A jolt of realization went through Kanvar, and the hair on his arms stood on end. *Dhar, you can see?*

Now Dharanidhar laughed full out as he shared with Kanvar the unlikely friendship he'd developed with Kivi. *That's brilliant,* Kanvar said. *Dharanidhar, I'm so happy for you.*

Yes, fine, be happy, but get back to work. You have to find Raahi.

Kanvar laughed out loud, hard enough that moisture rimmed the edges of his own eyes. Dharanidhar could see. He could see and hunt, fly and fight. It was the first little brightness of hope and happiness Kanvar had experienced in a long time.

"Did you find Raahi?" Lord Theodoric asked.

Kanvar choked back his laugher. "No. I'm sorry, no. It's just . . . my dragon has such a wondrous sense of humor." Kanvar brushed the moisture from his eyes. "I'm afraid I'm having trouble finding Raahi. There are too many people. I thought his mind would be bright for me. I've known him for so long, and we were so close."

"Perhaps he's not in the city then. You said he lived in one of the villages up the river."

"Yes, you're right, but even at this distance in Kundiland I can pick out the minds of anyone I know. There are just so many more people here."

"Let me help you," Lord Theodoric said, giving Kanvar's shoulder a squeeze. "I'm used to sorting through thousands of minds. You ask me if I can heal, and I say that is for the healers to do. You ask me if I can manipulate stone, and I say that is for the builders to do. Surely you've wondered what it is that I'm useful for."

Kanvar shrugged. The thought had occurred to him, but he'd kept it to himself.

"I am the Lord of Navgarod, ruler of Aesir. Keeping track of people, both humans and Nagas, and seeing to their welfare is my duty. Show me what your friend's mind feels like, and I will find him for you."

Relieved, Kanvar showed Lord Theodoric the memories he had of Raahi. The five years Raahi had served as General Samdrasen's slave while Kanvar had done the same as Chandran's indentured servant. Raahi had been Kanvar's friend when Kanvar had no other. Kanvar missed him and was not anxious to draw Raahi into the war with Khalid. He preferred to think Raahi could live safely forever in his mountain village with his father, mother, and little brother.

"That's helpful," Lord Theodoric said. "Not just your friend but his family as well. I've found them. Ishayu fly upriver. They're in the village farthest from Huayna along the river."

Ishayu left Huayna behind and followed the river up into the heart of the mountains. The sky had warmed to full brightness by the time Raahi's village came into view on the side of a crescent-shaped arm of the mountain. Terraces of green crops led up to a cluster of stone houses.

"Amazing," Lord Theodoric said, taking in the stonework of the buildings. The Darvati stonemasons were the best architects in the world, and even this tiny village showed a wondrous array of stonework from raised balustrades and arches to carved friezes that would put to shame even the wealthiest houses in Daro.

"Raahi's father, Stonebiter, is one of the best stonemasons who ever lived. I assume the big house there at the top of the village is his," Kanvar said. The house was a dazzling array of levels and wings that clung to the mountain as if the stone was a natural outgrowth of the rock itself.

Ishayu swooped toward it to land.

"No, wait," Kanvar said. "Stay back. Raahi knows I'm a Naga, but the other villagers don't. They're not as hostile to Nagas as most humans because Karishi has watched over them for so long, but we should be cautious. Land away from the village and we'll walk to his house."

"I've been wondering," Lord Theodoric said as Ishayu landed on a bit of the hill away from the village. "With so few Nagas anywhere on this side of the world, how Karishi could come to be here all by himself."

"I don't know." Kanvar slid off the dragon and started limping toward the village. The ground was steep, and he wished he had a spear or something to steady himself as he tried to get down the slope. "Karishi said he was abandoned on the mountain as a newborn. He never knew his parents."

Lord Theodoric came alongside Kanvar and wrapped an arm under his shoulders to steady him as they traversed the steep slope. The villagers had carved stairs in the mountain everywhere they usually went, but Ishayu had not landed by any of those. Kanvar thought about pulling away and insisting he could navigate the slope by himself but thought better of it. He'd chided LaShawn about pride and figured he'd better keep his own in check. Who knew how much time he had before the other Nagas arrived.

"Precisely," Lord Theodoric said. "Infant Nagas do not appear out of nowhere in the middle of the Darvat mountains. But let's say you were a human father and found out your daughter had secretly married a Naga. LaShawn did not say his wife had been with child when she was taken from him, so it must have been too soon to tell, but I'm thinking perhaps she was, and the baby was left to die because of who his father was."

"You think LaShawn is Karishi's father?" Kanvar said, surprised. That thought had not occurred to him. "I think Karishi would be delighted to learn his father is still alive, and he could meet him."

"If LaShawn ever chooses to leave his home."

"Perhaps he would if he knew."

As Lord Theodoric and Kanvar neared the village, a cry of surprise went up from a group of girls who were washing clothes beside a cistern. No one came down from above the village, strangers always arrived coming up the steps from below. The girls abandoned their washing and ran in among the houses to rouse the rest of the villagers.

"That was friendly," Lord Theodoric said, sarcastically.

Kanvar chuckled, but his muscles went tense. *I hope they don't figure out we're Nagas*, he said in his mind to Theodoric.

They have no reason to think we are, Theodoric answered. As soon as they got off the slope and onto the steps, he let go so Kanvar could walk on his own. By the time they reached the houses, the steps were lined with men, women, and children all along the path to Stonebiter's house. If strangers came to the village, they always came to see the Great Stonebiter.

Stonebiter's elaborately carved door swung open and Raahi's little brother, Tiago, burst out. "Kanvar," he shouted and raced over to hug Kanvar's legs.

Kanvar greeted the boy then looked up to see Stonebiter and Raahi come out of the house. Upon seeing Kanvar, a grin lit up Raahi's face.

"Kanvar." He strode down the steps and clasped Kanvar's hands in greeting. "It's good to see you. I was beginning to think you would never keep your promise and come visit me."

"Sorry, Raahi. I've been off with my grandfather hunting a Great Red volcanic dragon."

"Are you crazy?"

"Kumar Raza is. It was his idea. He just dragged me along for the fun of it."

"I suppose he succeeded in killing the dragon?" Raahi shook his head in amazement.

"Yes, of course. Raahi, this is Theodoric, a friend my grandfather made during his most recent travels. He has business here in Darvat, so I brought him along."

"Welcome to Darvat." Stonebiter descended the stairs from his front door and shook Lord Theodoric's hand. "What business brings you here? Perhaps I can be of service."

Keep him busy, so I can speak with Raahi alone, Kanvar told Lord Theodoric.

Yes, of course. "My mansion was seriously damaged in a recent earthquake, and when Kumar Raza told me of your skills, I had to come see you. I doubt you will want to travel halfway around the world to oversee the rebuilding of my home, but I thought you might be able to help me with some ideas on how to repair the damage in a way that would be more structurally sound than the original."

"Most certainly," Stonebiter said, clapping Theodoric on the back. "Come on in."

"Hey, Tiago," Raahi said. "Why don't you go in and show Theodoric your rock collection? I'm sure he'll be amazed."

Tiago let out a shout of excitement and rushed into the house. Raahi smiled fondly as he watched his brother leave. Then he sat down on the terrace wall around his father's property. "Kanvar, I know you too well, and I don't like the look in your eyes. You're mouth is smiling, but you aren't happy."

"I am glad to see you."

"What's wrong?"

Kanvar waited for the last of the villagers to go back to their regular tasks before answering. When they were gone, he explained to Raahi everything that had happened leading up to Khalid's return, and how the singing stones were gone and the human world doomed to slavery unless something could be found to stop the Nagas.

Raahi's face went from its usual tan to a sickening white as Kanvar spoke. "My people will be enslaved again?"

"Yes. This is not an enemy Bolivar or my grandfather can fight without singing stones." Kanvar knew this topic was delicate. He could not just demand his friend show him to the Hall of His Ancestors and allow him to chisel the gems from the walls.

Raahi bit his lip. His fingers clenched the stone wall. Kanvar waited for him to speak, but he said nothing.

"I've thought about this a lot, Raahi, and it occurred to me that your people believe the spirits of your ancestors watch over and protect this land. If that is their main calling and purpose, do you think any of them might volunteer to leave the mountain and join your father and Bolivar in keeping your people's minds free from Naga control?"

"You know what you're asking?" Raahi's voice sounded like stone grinding on stone.

"I know that your ancestors must be made to understand they will experience unspeakable torment while they are away from the Hall. It has to be their own choice, Raahi. They must join the battle against Khalid willingly. And you and I would have to promise them on our souls that when it is over, we will return them to peace in the Hall." Kanvar held his breath. Raahi was the protector of the Hall, and Kanvar was asking him to betray all his oaths and purpose.

Raahi pressed his head into his hands and sat in silence, speaking with his ancestors perhaps. Kanvar kept his own mind separate so as not to interrupt. Finally, Raahi sighed and looked up at Kanvar. "There are some who are willing. Not many. But it doesn't matter. Karishi sealed the mountain. Neither you nor I could get to it. It would take a week for our best miners to cut through the stone, and then everyone would know about the Hall. I can't let that happen. If only you had brought Karishi with you."

A spark of hope welled up in Kanvar. Raahi was going to be reasonable about this. "Karishi was too far away, so I brought his grandfather."

"What?"

"Theodoric. I have reason to believe he is Karishi's grandfather. Whether or not that turns out to be true, Theodoric can open the mountain."

"He's a Naga too then?" Red crept up Raahi's neck into his face.

"Yes. Does that bother you?" Kanvar sensed his friend's unease but wasn't sure how to soothe it.

Raahi's hands clenched into fists. Then he let out a deep breath and relaxed. "I suppose not. If you and Kumar Raza trust him, then I can try to trust him as well. But he has to take an oath that he will take no gems from the Hall except the ones I tell him to, and that he will never reveal its existence to anyone."

"I made him swear before I brought him anywhere near here," Kanvar said.

"Very well then." Raahi jumped up from the wall. "We have a bit of a hike ahead of us. I know I can make it without any problem. You, on the other hand, no offense, might have a hard time of it."

"I'll do fine if you can get me a spear or something with a handle so I can steady myself."

"A walking stick. Of course. The old grandfathers use them." Raahi flushed. "Sorry, Kanvar."

"I'm not offended. See if you can borrow one from somebody and let's get going."

"All right." Raahi chuckled. "I'll ask my mother to pack us some food and get the walking stick while you pry

Theodoric away from my father. Good luck with that if he's got him really going on house design."

Laughing, Kanvar limped up the steps to the house with Raahi. But the back of his neck prickled, and he turned to scan the sky before going in, searching for the ripples of gold dragon flight, sending his senses out in search of the Nagas he knew were coming after him. Ishayu would be able to fly all three of them to the head of the river so much faster. Perhaps after they got out of sight of the village, he'd be able to convince Raahi he wanted to take a ride on a gold dragon. The day was already wasting away. If he had to walk, the other Nagas might get there first.

Chapter Sixteen

Amar kissed Mani goodbye and followed the other Nagas up out of the mountain. He'd cleaned the second jungle knife and given it to Tana so the set could be together in her hands. He did not like that Kumar Raza's battle plans included Tana and Vasanti, but Kumar had insisted Vasanti's part was vital and Tana would not be in the middle of the battle. She and Vasanti had left the mountain earlier to be in place when the time was right.

The heat and humidity of the jungle washed over Amar as he stepped out of the mountain. Stars still glimmered overhead but were already starting to fade into the half-light before dawn. He felt strange in his new armor, though it fit him more comfortably than several of the outfits he had back at the palace. He never would have guessed something like it could be fashioned out of metal.

He curled his hand into a fist and watched the segmented gold plates move along with him as if he'd been born in the skin of a gold dragon. The smell of gold hung on him now as it always had with Rajahansa. He cringed and shoved thoughts of Rajahansa aside as he went to Bensharie.

Bensharie bowed. *Good morning, Your Majesty.*

"Morning, Bensharie." He rubbed Bensharie's neck. "Are you ready to fly?"

Sensing Amar's trepidation about the coming battle, Bensharie said, *Maybe the Nagas will listen to you, and we won't have to fight at all.*

"I hope so. Lord Theodoric accepts me as the king, but he didn't think many of the others will. It would be nice not to have to fight them." Amar handed an iron spear to Bensharie and climbed on his back.

Dharanidhar swooped down to land on the ledge and drink the medicine the villagers had strapped in a barrel to the transport platform. When he was done drinking, he lifted Rajan up onto his back. Rajan buckled himself in place with a harness like the one Kanvar used. Rajan's eyes were cold and fierce and his thoughts locked away from Amar's.

"Ready?" Kumar Raza stopped beside Bensharie. Raza carried his sword at his side, his crossbow and two of Karishi's spears strapped across his back, and a new red helmet in his hand that Karishi had made for him.

"I don't like this," Amar said. "If they won't listen to me, we may have to hurt or kill someone." That was the last thing Amar wanted to do.

Kumar Raza's jaw tightened. "Several someones. But who would you rather have die, armed soldiers or innocent women and children?"

"I don't want anyone to die."

"Right." Kumar's hand tightened on the helmet. "Just do what we planned. Got it?"

Amar frowned down at him. Like Rajan's mind, Kumar Raza's was shielded from him. General Chandran strode over, carrying a new helmet as well, though his was painted blue to match his armor. "What's the problem?"

"His Majesty doesn't want to kill anyone. Come on." Kumar Raza motioned for Dharanidhar to pick him up in his claw.

General Chandran was armed the same as Kumar Raza. "No good soldier *wants* to kill," he told Amar. "I'd certainly like to see my men down in that garrison come out of this unscathed. But it's your duty as a husband and father to protect your family, and as a man to defend the freedom of this world. If that means taking another man's life in battle, then that is what you have to do."

Amar kept his own shield up so stray thoughts from General Chandran's mind couldn't slip in. He didn't like being so cut off from the people he had to work with. Of the group, only Dharanidhar was tightly linked to his mind so the Great Blue dragon could hear every word of Amar's conversations and know whether to attack or not.

"I get the feeling you've given that speech before," Amar said to Chandran.

General Chandran rested his crossbow on his shoulder. "I've trained a lot of young soldiers. Stop analyzing this, Amar. The time for thinking and planning is over. You must act."

Amar nodded, though his blood felt thick as tree sap pumping through his heart.

Dharanidhar scooped up General Chandran in his other foreclaw and took flight.

I can quote some poetry to you if it will make you feel better, Bensharie said as he flapped away from the cliff.

"Please don't." Amar said.

Kanvar likes my poetry.

"Save it for later."

The sky had turned gray by the time the Maran Colony with its volcanic rock walls came into view. The Naga Guardsmen and soldiers had once again turned it into the fortress that had withstood blue dragon attack for decades. A tower with spyglasses and a warning bell rose up in the center. Heavy ballistae were mounted on all four walls and manned by soldiers even at this early hour. The entire Great Blue dragon pride had never succeeded in defeating the humans housed there. *And we just have Dharanidhar,* Amar thought.

Not just Dharanidhar, Bensharie answered. *We have General Chandran, Rajan and—*

"I know. Stop talking. Let's just get this over with."

Right. Bensharie winged toward the front gate of the fortress.

A cry went up and the bell started to toll. Bensharie stopped and flapped in place just outside of what General Chandran had said was ballista range. Amar felt the Nagas stir from sleep and become aware of the bell. He waited while they pulled themselves together, mounted their dragons, and took to the air.

Five Nagas and five gold dragons, fully visible in the predawn light, rose into the air and fanned out, two on each side of a central man. The Naga in the center wore a golden vest over a white silk shirt. His golden hair was tied back with a diamond-studded leather thong. He carried both crossbow and sword. A startled look crossed his face for a moment as he realized the enemy he faced was riding a gold dragon and must be a Naga.

My name is Captain Vitra, the man said to Amar's mind since the distance between them was too far for vocal conversation. *King Khalid has placed me in command of this continent. Name yourself and swear on oath to my service and fealty to the king.*

I am the king, Amar said. *Amar, grandson of Khalid, rightful heir to the throne. And I call you and your men into my service.* Amar spoke so Vitra and the other Nagas could hear.

Vitra's dragon back-flapped in surprise. Vitra's mind spun for a moment until he brought it back under tight control. *I was told King Khalid's grandson was bound to Rajahansa, and Rajahansa's death has been confirmed. It will do you no good pretending to be the king.*

If you examined Rajahansa's body, then you will recognize the wounds that killed him. Amar let Bensharie fly up closer to Captain Vitra so Vitra and his men could get a clear view of Bensharie's body. *Like Nikeron of old, I bonded with a new dragon at the time of Rajahansa's death. The wounds just before the killing blow manifested on myself and Bensharie. See for yourself. I am Amar.*

Captain Vitra's face went scarlet. "I don't care if you are Amar," he shouted. "Khalid is the king and has right to his throne before any grandson."

Khalid is dead and his right to the throne died with him. If he has taken the body of my son, then he is still second in line to the throne after me as my son would be. I command you to surrender this fortress and swear fealty to me. Amar held his breath, pleading by the fountain that Captain Vitra would accept him as the rightful king.

The other four Nagas flew in closer to get a look at Bensharie. Behind them, Vasanti climbed the colony walls and sent her tail slithering over the side to paralyze the men arming the ballistae that faced Amar's direction. On the opposite wall, Silverwave unmanned the other ballistae by dragging the soldiers two at a time down into the ocean before they had a chance to shout. Along the wall next to the river, Indumauli did the same.

I see no reason to swear fealty to you, Captain Vitra said. *You are no kind of a king. You are a coward who has done nothing but hide in this hole of a jungle for centuries. You had the power to take control of this world, and you didn't even try. I will not serve you. Khalid is my king, always has been and always will be.*

Amar sighed. He could feel the iron spear Bensharie had gripped in his foreclaw. He did not want to have to use it. *What about the rest of you?* he asked the other Nagas. *You have the choice of embracing the tyranny and vile perversions of Khalid or joining me in trying to stop him. What say you?*

In the blue-gray light, Amar could barely make out Dharanidhar winging in from the ocean above the remaining ship in the bay, his body blending with water and sky. The men on the watch tower did not sound the bell again; their full gaze was fixed on the confrontation between Amar and the Nagas.

Kanvar was glad Raahi had accepted the opportunity to ride a Great Gold dragon. His friend's face had beamed with excitement as Ishayu hoisted him up on his neck along with Lord Theodoric. Kanvar was glad to see his friend so happy and didn't mind riding in Ishayu's claw instead of up with Theodoric.

Raahi gave Theodoric directions, and Ishayu flew to the river and followed it northward until it ended in a pool of water below a cliff face. When Kanvar caught sight of the cliff, a sense of foreboding and wonder took him. It was so much like the side of the mountain at Stonefountain where the great palace now stood crumbling. But more, it was very like the cliff in Kundiland where the new golden palace had been built at the head of yet another river.

My Lord, Kanvar asked as Ishayu spiraled down to land beside the pool at Raahi's bidding. *Is there a river by your city in Navgarod?*

Yes, of course. You can't build a city without some source of fresh water.

Ishayu set Kanvar down and lowered himself to the ground so Raahi and Theodoric could dismount.

"Have you ever been to the head of it?" Kanvar asked aloud now the two of them were close enough to speak.

Lord Theodoric looked perplexed. "I'm sure I've been that way once or twice but never made a point of exploring all the way to the source. Why?"

Kanvar rubbed the hairs that were prickling on the back of his neck. "There's a river that runs past the Maran capital, too, that comes out from the heart of their central mountain range."

"You have to have water, Kanvar," Theodoric said. Raahi handed him the basket of food his mother had prepared for them.

Kanvar's stomach growled. In his hurry to get underway that morning he had not eaten breakfast, and it was already nearing noon. He hoped Raahi's mother was a good cook. The smells coming from the basket hinted that perhaps she was.

"Of course you have to have water," Kanvar said. "But, we know, because Khalid was there, that Stonefountain houses the spirits of the dead from the old city. We also know the Hall of Raahi's Ancestors houses the spirits of the dead from this land because he saw his sister there. If that's the case, where do all the other spirits go when people die?"

Raahi spread a rainbow-colored blanket on the ground and pulled the food out of the basket—hot bovinder pies, fresh strawberries, and a jug of what Raahi's mother had called the family's best sweet-berry cider. "Maybe spirits from the whole world went to Stonefountain until Stonefountain fell, then they all started coming here," Raahi said. "In any case, what you're looking for is inside that cliff. Unless you're very good at climbing, Ishayu will have to fly up and hover beside it while Theodoric opens the way."

"There's no way I could climb up that," Lord Theodoric said, shading his eyes to look at the shear cliff. "We should eat quickly though. Who knows when Khalid's men will catch up with us." Theodoric sat down, grabbed a pie, and accepted a cup of cider, which he drank quickly and poured himself another.

Kanvar hesitated. His feeling of foreboding grew stronger. "Or, every continent has its own fountain of power. We just haven't gone looking for them." Still staring at the cliff, he sat down and accepted the cup of cider Raahi handed him. It was just the right amount of sweet and quenched Kanvar's thirst. "Mmm, that is good" he said, sipping at the sweet drink.

"That's a scary thought," Lord Theodoric said. "Do you know what that would mean, Kanvar? If the humans found out, no Naga would be safe anywhere. The humans could pick up singing stones all over the place and murder Nagas at will." Frowning, Lord Theodoric leaned back and put his hands behind his head.

Kanvar lay down on the blanket and stared up into the sky as a fuzzy sense of rightness crept over him. "I think that would make the world safe and fair. If the fountains are the source of Naga power, then it makes sense the fountains would also be the source that can hold that power in check."

"At the expense of the spirits of the dead," Raahi said, jumping to his feet. Red washed his face. "That is a horrible thought, Kanvar. The dead must be left in peace."

"Yes, of course." Kanvar's mind sank into a mire of lassitude. Above him the sky began to ripple. The ripples circled above him and sank down toward the pool. Khalid's Nagas, he thought long moments after it should have occurred to him.

A jolt of fear went through him, but when he tried to jump up, he found his body numb and unresponsive.

"Raahi," he said, too weak to speak in more than a whisper. "What have you done?"

Raahi glared down at him. "Devaj came here a while after he'd taken Karishi away. He said you had grown greedy and wanted the gems from the Hall to adorn your palace, but no matter what you said I wasn't to let you have them. He gave me the elixir I put in the cider." Raahi pulled a strand of rope from the basket and bound Kanvar's good arm and legs. Then tied Lord Theodoric as well.

Theodoric's eyes were closed and he made no move to resist.

By the fountain, Kanvar thought, Khalid has already been here. Vaguely he remembered Devaj saying he had gone to Darvat to check on Raahi while Kanvar was on the other side of the world. Khalid had foreseen Kanvar coming here and made Devaj come to set this trap long before Kanvar even thought about using the stones from the Hall against him.

Kanvar groaned. Khalid had taken control of Raahi's mind.

Raahi got a strip of cloth, soaked it in the cider, and used it to gag Kanvar. The berry juice was still sweat and pleasant, so innocent tasting as it spread across his mouth. He heard the flap of dragon wings directly overhead just before his eyesight went dark. *It's a trap*, he screamed to Dharanidhar then fell unconscious.

Chapter Seventeen

Amar looked past the five Nagas in the air in front of him as Dharanidhar glided up behind their backs into crossbow range. Both General Chandran and Kumar Raza had a damp cloth tied over their mouth and nose to filter out gold dragon joy breath. Their weapons were loaded ready to fire.

Amar's hand clenched on his sword. By the fountain, please, he thought, let the Naga Guardsmen join me. I don't want anyone to die. Captain Vitra was already a target. Dharanidhar had heard his declaration of loyalty to Khalid and passed it on to Rajan who told the other men. Kumar Raza's crossbow was pointed directly at Captain Vitra's back, and Amar had hunted long enough with Kumar Raza to know he seldom missed.

The Nagas looked nervously between Captain Vitra and Amar.

Will you join me? Amar asked again.

Three of them shook their heads and reached for their crossbows. The man on the far right glanced away and said nothing. Amar sensed fear of Vitra and confusion rolling off him. There might be a chance for that one. The others . . . Amar couldn't bring himself to give the order to shoot them down. But Kumar Raza had never given him the option of deciding whether to attack or not. The moment the Nagas reached for their crossbows, General Chandran and Kumar Raza fired their weapons. Both bolts would have flown true, but Dharanidhar groaned and lurched to the side. His sudden movement spoiled Chandran's and Kumar's aim.

Through Amar's link with Dharanidhar, he felt the blue dragon's mind spin and his body go slack. *It's a trap*, Kanvar cried across the distance, but his voice was only a fuzzy whisper, fading to silence.

Dharanidhar's wings went limp and he fell. His forward momentum sent him crashing into the lookout tower. His massive body tore off the top of the tower. The bell gave a loud desperate gong, crashed to the ground, and rolled away as Dharanidhar skidded to a stop in the square.

"Kill them!" Captain Vitra shouted to his men and pointed to General Chandran, Kumar Raza, and Rajan who were scrambling away from Dharanidhar and up onto the tower platform that remained roofless and without its bell. "I'll take care of this pretend king."

Green flashed from the colony wall toward the tower as Vasanti with Tana curled in her tail launched herself across the buildings to the square where the human soldiers converged toward Dharanidhar. General Chandran and Kumar Raza slipped their helmets on, and the sense of their presence vanished from Amar's mind.

Captain Vitra's dragon lunged tooth and claw toward Bensharie. The size and force of his body tore Bensharie from the sky and flung him on the ground just outside the city gate. The impact knocked Amar from his seat on Bensharie's back, and he rolled clear of the struggling dragons.

Though Vitra's dragon had Bensharie pinned to the ground, Bensharie thrashed to free himself and let out a spurt of joy breath, hoping to hit Vitra. The joy breath would do nothing to a gold dragon directly, but would stop the Naga and affect the dragon indirectly.

Telanies, Captain Vitra's dragon, roared and lifted his head out of range to avoid the glittering air. The move let Bensharie get his forearms in position to rake the iron spear he carried across Telanies's chest. It was a feeble blow, but the shock of it made Telanies pull back off Bensharie and lick his chest. The wound did not close. Blood soaked the front of Captain Vitra's shirt and vest. He screamed in pain and outrage, slid from his dragon's back, and came after Amar, drawing his sword.

Amar scrambled to his feet and pulled the sword Rajan had given him from its sheath. Amar could not see what was happening in the colony except for the tower platform that rose up above the height of the walls. Four gold dragons closed in on it, breathing joy breath while their Nagas shot their crossbows at the three defenders.

Kumar Raza's crossbow answered in response. The closest Naga to the tower doubled over as the bolt pierced his heart. Dragon and Naga fell. Amar felt the Naga's spirit tear free from his body and vanish, leaving the pain of an empty place in Amar's heart.

Captain Vitra's sword flashed toward Amar's neck. Amar flinched and twisted to the side so the sword clanged against his steel helm. The force of the blow made his ears ring and knocked him off balance so he stumbled to the side.

Fight him, Bensharie shouted. *Use the sword.* Bensharie was locked in battle with Telanies, though Telanies kept his distance now, wary of the iron spear Bensharie wielded.

Amar managed to get his sword in position to block Vitra's next blow. "I-I don't want to kill you," Amar said, taking up what he hoped was a fighting stance.

"Don't worry, I don't see how that is likely to happen," Captain Vitra said, advancing a step. "Have you ever even used a sword before?"

Amar edged back, watching Vitra's hands so he could block the next sword strike. "Only for the bonding ceremony and on hunts of lesser dragons."

Captain Vitra laughed and lunged forward, stabbing at Amar's heart. Once more his sword dented Amar's armor. Amar's late block came only in time to push the blade away after it hit.

"You are pathetic," Vitra said, swinging into a series of thrusts and slices that drove Amar backward and made contact with his armor as often as his blade.

Above the colony, one of the gold dragons pulled away from the tower. Rajan had somehow gotten up on its back and was attacking the Naga with his claws. The Naga let out a gurgling scream and fell silent.

The pain of the Naga's death tore Amar apart. He stumbled and fell. Captain Vitra came down on top of him, pinning Amar's sword arm with his knee. Vitra tore the helm from Amar's head and pressed his sword against Amar's throat.

Amar gasped, he could see in Vitra's mind that he intended to kill him. He would have no mercy. He was savoring the moment, enjoying Amar's terror.

"There's no other dragon for you to bond with this time," Vitra said. "This time you die and stay dead."

Amar's left hand closed on the hunting knife Kumar Raza had given him back at the new village. He pulled it out and thrust it into Vitra's gut.

Vitra cried out in surprise and looked down at the knife handle protruding from his body. *Telanies,* he screamed. *Heal me.*

Telanies turned away from Bensharie to come to his Naga's aid. Bensharie took advantage of the moment. Clasping the spear with both hands, he flew at Telanies's chest and thrust the spear in with the full momentum of his body behind it. The spear plunged through Telanies's protective plates and struck his heart. Telanies roared and thrashed, tearing at the spear for a moment before collapsing in death.

Captain Vitra fell dead beside Amar.

"No," Amar cried as another Naga's soul was ripped from the world.

Bensharie flapped over to him. The little gold dragon was shaking. Gashes from Telanies's claws marred his body. Amar felt the pain. Beneath his armor, he too must be bleeding, but Bensharie licked his own wounds closed, healing both of them.

Only one Naga remained in the air now. Chandran and Kumar must have succeeded in bringing down the others. Amar felt the sense of the Nagas' loss and pressed a hand against his heart. Too much death. Too much killing.

I surrender, the last Naga cried into Amar's mind. *Please, spare me.*

Amar looked up and realized that Rajan was once again a passenger on a gold dragon, which had flown out over the river away from Kumar Raza and General Chandran. Rajan had his claws to the Naga's throat, but the Naga had thrown down his weapons and begged to be spared. He was the one who had been undecided about which king he should follow.

Rajan, stop! Amar shouted, but Rajan's mind was all bloodlust and hunger to kill.

Amar grabbed hold of Rajan's mind and jerked it away from thoughts of murder and the taste of human flesh. *Release him*, Amar ordered. *Let him go.*

Rajan came back to himself suddenly. His mind filled with shock and revulsion at himself. He let go of the Naga and dove from the gold dragon's back. With a splash, Silverwave jumped from the river, caught Rajan in her coils, and glided back down to disappear beneath the water.

Come here, Amar called to the remaining Naga.

Naga and dragon landed beside the fallen Telanies.

Picking up his sword, Amar kept his eyes averted from Captain Vitra's dead body. Just the thought of it made him light headed. He stumbled away and turned his back on the dead. Inside the colony, he could feel Tana releasing General Chandran's men from the orders Captain Vitra had placed in their minds. Vasanti had been struck by several crossbow bolts in defense of the fallen Dharanidhar, but none had been a killing blow and the Great Green dragon had already licked the wounds closed.

"Forgive me, Your Majesty." The Naga came around to face Amar and dropped to his knees. He bowed his head. "I pledge myself to your service and swear fealty to you as king." The man was still undecided if this was the right and honorable course of action. He did not know if he was betraying his Lord and the rightful king or not, but in the face of death it appeared to be his only option.

"Lord Theodoric has pledged himself to me as well," Amar said, hoping to dispel the man's worries. "What is your name?"

"I am Lieutenant Walinash, Your Majesty. Has My Lord truly joined you?"

"Yes, he has. I have sent him on an important mission." Amar swallowed. With Dharanidhar unconscious in the town square, Amar could only assume Kanvar and Theodoric had failed. But Dharanidhar was not dead, Amar could not read his darkened mind, but he was close enough he could feel his living body. Kanvar had said it was a trap. That meant that Kanvar and Theodoric were most likely back in Khalid's hands as prisoners, and the singing stones would not be accessible except through another bloody battle. How long, Amar wondered, would Khalid let Kanvar or Lord Theodoric live?

Bensharie, are you well enough to fly me to Kumar Raza? He needs to know what happened, Amar said.

I can fly, Bensharie said. He flapped over to Amar and let him climb on his back, then took to the air and headed for the square in the center of the colony where Kumar Raza and General Chandran stood on the platform addressing General Chandran's soldiers.

Bensharie settled onto the platform.

Kumar Raza pulled off his helmet and gave Amar a hand down. "You look a bit worse for the wear. It might take Karishi a while to hammer out all those dents in your armor. My apologies, we had agreed you would not have to fight, and I failed you." Kumar Raza looked down at the fallen Dharanidhar. "I had the prefect shot. I don't understand what happened."

Feeling sick, Amar told Kumar Raza about Kanvar's last message and the likely meaning behind it.

Kumar Raza swore. "I'm tired of always being two steps behind Khalid. But don't worry. We'll go after Kanvar and Theodoric and free them."

"How? The only dragon we have now is Bensharie," Amar said.

Kumar Raza's gaze flicked out to where Walinash knelt beside Captain Vitra, easing the hunting knife from his body. Walinash's dragon stood nearby, shading his Naga with his wings.

"What about that one," Kumar Raza said. "You made Rajan spare him for a reason, I assume."

"He surrendered and has sworn fealty to me."

"Can you trust him?"

"I don't know. He's conflicted."

Kumar Raza picked up a bloody spear, wiped it clean, and slid it into the harness on his back. "Give me your spear," he said to General Chandran.

Chandran broke off talking to two of his men who had climbed up on the tower. He pulled his remaining spear from his harness and handed it to Kumar Raza. Kumar thanked him.

"What's going on?" Chandran asked.

Kumar checked his crossbow and his sword without answering. "Amar, call your man over here. General Chandran," Kumar looked the general hard in the face. "Can I count on you to remain loyal to our cause until Khalid is dead?"

"You know you can count on me," General Chandran said, scowling.

"I want your oath that you will not try to harm Amar, Tana, Rajan, or any of the Nagas that join our side while I'm away."

"You're going somewhere?"

Amar called Walinash to join them on the tower.

"Your Majesty," General Chandran took off his helmet and spoke before Walinash landed. "I swear that I will keep you and your people safe here. My men have agreed to this alliance and are thankful that you have freed their minds. I . . . I was wrong about you. Kanvar tried to tell me about your goodness and the respect you have for human life and freedom, and I didn't believe him. But I've been watching you, judging you, waiting for you to show your true evil since we met at the village. You've shown your true self at every turn, and I find myself surprised. Kanvar was right. You are a good man. I could not have hoped for a better ally against Khalid . . . even if you can't fight worth a pile of camdor droppings. Fortunately, your dragon seems to make up for that weakness."

General Chandran grinned at Bensharie and turned back to Kumar Raza. "Satisfied?"

"Thank you." Kumar Raza clasped General Chandran's arm. "You there," he said to Walinash. "His Majesty believes your Lord has been captured. Want to join me in a campaign to free him and His Majesty's son?"

Walinash paled. "I will go where His Majesty sends me." He looked to Amar for orders.

"You're the only person I have to send, Lieutenant. I need you to do this. Take Kumar Raza with you and follow his orders. If anyone can save them from Khalid, it's him."

"I will gladly follow your command, Majesty."

Amar sensed from Walinash's mind that he was indeed glad to be sent with Kumar Raza instead of staying around Rajan. Rajan had instilled in him a mindless terror. Amar was surprised to realize Rajan had not just been fighting with his teeth and claws, but also with his mind. He'd gotten up onto the gold dragons by breaking through their shields and tearing into their minds to control them. Amar shuddered. "I'm going to have to talk to Rajan about that."

Kumar Raza put a restraining hand on his shoulder. "It was a battle, Amar. When you face enemies that intend to kill you, you must use whatever weapon you can to win. Rajan's use of his powers was no different than your stabbing Captain Vitra with that hunting knife. It's a war, Amar. We have to win at whatever cost."

"Not if that cost makes us as bad as Khalid or worse." The pressure on Amar's heart would not ease. Bensharie came up beside him and put a wing around his shoulders.

"Rajan is nothing like Khalid. My brother did not want to fight or kill any more than you did, Amar, and he regretted it after. You don't see him here gloating over the dead, do you? No, he is off trying to recover some sense of peace and rightness, just like you are." Kumar Raza climbed up onto the gold dragon's neck behind Walinash. "Goodbye, my friend. Stay alive and guard those we love that are here. I'll save Kanvar. I promise."

Kumar Raza urged Walinash's dragon into the air. Amar watched them go, his fists clenched and heart beating.

"You should be happy," General Chandran said. "We saved your villagers and secured a base for ourselves. This battle went well and we are victorious without losing anyone on our side. Even most of my men were spared thanks to Tana, her dragon, the black serpent, and the silver one. I never imagined a group of dragons could be so effective in neutralizing an enemy. I have been in very few battles where the death toll is so low."

Amar leaned up against Bensharie, grateful for the companionship of the young dragon. "You're right, General. Thank you. Bensharie, I think I'm ready to hear some poetry now."

My pleasure, Bensharie said, *but I hope you realize, Your Majesty, that someday a thousand years from now we will be the heroes that the poets praise in verse.*

"A thousand years," Amar murmured. "I just want to live to see tomorrow and hope it dawns a brighter day than today."

About The Author

Rebecca Shelley (Rebecca Lyn Shelley) is the author of over 30 published books including the bestselling **Smart-boys Club** series as well as the popular **Red Dragon Codex** and **Brass Dragon Codex**. She loves writing about dragons and is excited to be writing the **Dragonbound** series. Her **Aos Si** *trilogy* will thrill fans of YA Paranormal Romance. To learn more or contact her, visit her website http://www.rebeccashelley.com.

If you have enjoyed reading **Dragonbound VII: Gold Dragon**, Rebecca would love to have you post a review on the site where you purchased it.

Dragonbound VIII: Black Dragon Preview
By Rebecca Shelley

Prologue

Indumauli snaked up the Black River, leaving the Maran Colony behind. The battle there had been swift and decisive. He'd done his part, tearing the Maran soldiers from the walls on the river side of the colony and disarming them. Two of them he'd had to kill to protect his own life. A strike with his poisoned fangs had finished them almost instantly. He regretted their deaths only because His Majesty Amar did. The other six humans he'd left alive, and they'd rejoined their commander, General Chandran, in service to the king.

That had been in the morning just before sunrise. Now, the brutal sun had risen into the sky, sending its fire over the jungle. Indumauli swam along the bottom of the river where it could not reach him. With the sun up, the humans were energetic and planning, the jungle vibrant with life. But Indumauli was tired and anxious to return to the cool darkness of his lair.

He passed below the deserted jungle village. Well, not totally deserted. The dragon hunters that had attacked the golden palace were there—dangerous men, the bravest of their kind who had allowed the Great Blue dragons to carry them into the heart of a battle between the human armies and dragon armies to destroy Rajahansa who had sided with Khalid. These hunters were not to be trifled with. Indumauli was glad His Majesty Amar had not allowed Kumar Raza and Rajan to take control of their minds and use them in the attack against the Maran Colony.

Hidden from them in the depths of the river, Indumauli shuddered. They'd killed Rajahansa, Indumauli's king and long time friend. Sorrow like burning rays of sunshine swept through him. Rajahansa should not have had to die. Indumauli dug his webbed claws into the mud at the bottom of the river, digging out great gouges in anguish. *Rajahansa, Rajahansa, why did you turn against your own friends?* he implored the dead Great Gold Dragon King. *What could Khalid have promised you that would twist your heart against those of us who loved you most?*

He received no answer, for ghosts do not speak so easily.

In what place does your spirit rest, Indumauli wondered, *at Stonefountain? If I could find your stone, perhaps I could speak to you one last time, perhaps we could find some reconciliation.*

Only the hollow echo of the river's current responded.

Groaning, Indumauli flicked his body and sped up the underground tributary into the heart of the mountain beside the jungle village. He found Aadi waiting for him in his lair, dangling his feet into the lake Indumauli called home. He surfaced and rubbed his scaly head against Aadi's legs.

"Indumauli." Aadi slipped into the water beside him. "You're back. How did the battle go? Did you…win?"

We won, Indumauli said. He knew Aadi could not hear his words but the young man would understand ideas behind them.

Aadi kicked to the edge of the water and climbed up on shore. "Is anyone hurt?"

Vasanti and Bensharie were wounded but have healed. Indumauli crawled up beside Aadi and wrapped his coils around the boy. *I'm tired. Let me sleep now.*

Aadi shuddered. Indumauli could feel Aadi's torment had grown during the hours he'd been away. The boy was in the throes of an agonizing emptiness as if he were deep in the dragon fever, but his skin remained damp and cool.

"I'm going to die, Indumauli," he said. "I'm going to die if I can't get to the gold dragons. Being around them is the only chance I have that the fever may start. I was hoping . . ." Aadi didn't finish his thoughts out loud, but Indumauli sensed them in his mind. Aadi had hoped that the Nagas would side with Amar, and one of them would carry Aadi to the gold dragon pride at Stonefountain. So many of the gold dragons were his friends, he was sure they would hide him from Khalid, and he would get the fever and bond with one of them. Aadi's disappointment was as consuming as Indumauli's grief at losing Rajahansa.

Indumauli hissed and uncoiled from Aadi. *I want to go to Stonefountain as well.*

Aadi started in surprise. "You do? Why?"

To speak with Rajahansa's spirit. I cannot rest without some understanding between us. He felt I betrayed him, siding with Amar against him. But it was not him I fought against; it was Khalid. And it was not me who betrayed him in the end; it was Khalid. Can't you see, Aadi. I can find no peace here.

Aadi climbed to his feet. "But how will we get to Stonefountain? You can't fly."

I can swim, Indumauli said.

"In the ocean?"

The salt in the water stings my eyes and makes my scales itch. It will not be pleasant, but I can cross the ocean. But you...you cannot swim so far. A thought sparked in Indumauli's mind. Silverwave had swum around the world pulling Kumar Raza in a little boat. There were boats in the jungle village, and supplies left behind.

"That's brilliant." Aadi's hands clenched into fists and he looked around at the solid walls of the rock chamber that housed the lake. "I don't think His Majesty Amar would approve though, and I can't get out of this mountain without his permission. Still, he can't keep me locked down here forever. He'll have to let us out now that it is safe."

The dragon hunters are still in the village. His Majesty will have Karishi keep you down here as long as they are there. Indumauli slid into the water and swam in an agitated circle.

"Wait," Aadi said. "Indumauli, if the mountain is sealed how do you get in and out?"

There is an underground channel that leads from the lake to the Black River.

"Then you could take me out that way," Aadi said.

Indumauli shook his head. *Humans do not breathe under water.*

"I can hold my breath. If you carry me and swim at your top speed we could get free together. I can sneak into the village, get the boat, and we'll be gone. Just don't tell His Majesty where we are and what we're doing until it's too late for him to stop us." Aadi took a deep breath and glanced one more time around the dark chamber. "Please, Indumauli."

Indumauli shook away his desire for sleep. *We should go now. They won't expect me to be doing anything in the daytime besides sleeping in my lair. That will buy us time. Can you shield your mind from the king?*

"Yes. Parmver drilled me on that relentlessly. I miss him."

I miss him too. Come down into the water. Get a good breath of air. You're going to need it.

Aadi slid into the lake beside Indumauli and sucked air into his lungs as Indumauli wrapped his coils around him. When he was ready, Indumauli dove beneath the surface, taking Aadi with him.